I0678650

The Wrestler

The Wrestler

A NOVEL

by
David Heddendorf

RESOURCE *Publications* • Eugene, Oregon

THE WRESTLER
A Novel

Copyright © 2021 David Heddendorf. All rights reserved. Except for brief quotations in critical publications or reviews, no part of this book may be reproduced in any manner without prior written permission from the publisher. Write: Permissions, Wipf and Stock Publishers, 199 W. 8th Ave., Suite 3, Eugene, OR 97401.

Resource Publications
An Imprint of Wipf and Stock Publishers
199 W. 8th Ave., Suite 3
Eugene, OR 97401

www.wipfandstock.com

PAPERBACK ISBN: 978-1-6667-0913-1
HARDCOVER ISBN: 978-1-6667-0914-8
EBOOK ISBN: 978-1-6667-0915-5

And Jacob was left alone. And a man wrestled with him
until the breaking of the day.

—GENESIS 32:24 (ESV)

Contents

I.

KNOWING

IN THE LITTLE HALLWAY at the top of the stairs, while playing with his green car that looked just like Daddy's, Mattie stopped and asked Jesus to come into his heart. He whispered the words that Mommy told him, because he was ready and he meant it. "Just say, 'Jesus, please come into my heart,'" Mommy had said. "But you have to really mean it. If you mean it, Jesus will come and live in your heart." Matty had listened with his head next to Mommy's soft side. She stroked the curls beside his ear. He would wait until it was time.

The hard floor hurt his knees a little, but the wood felt smooth against his forehead and his folded hands. He waited a few minutes, listening. Mommy's ironing board squeaked downstairs. The steam whooshed and sighed. Jesus didn't say anything, and Matty's heart felt the same. He was happy though, like after he drew the picture of the ladybug climbing the telephone pole. Mrs. Thompson said it was a pretty picture, so he drew more ladybugs until the grownups told him he should draw something else. But he knew the ladybug was his best.

He didn't tell Mommy or Daddy what happened. He wanted to make sure he'd really meant it. When Mommy woke him the next day he could tell that Jesus was still in his heart, so he knew it would be all right. He got dressed for school by himself, and went down to the kitchen where Mommy and Daddy were eating breakfast. Daddy gave him a little smile. Mommy rested her hand on his head while she poured milk on his cereal. Mattie bowed his head and whispered, "God is great, God is good, and we thank him for our food." He looked up. Daddy was reading the newspaper. Mommy was cooking bacon on the stove.

"Well, I did it," said Mattie.

He told them. Daddy smiled and looked proud. Mommy gave him a hug. Then they went back to the newspaper and the bacon. Mattie wondered if something else might happen. Maybe he would get a present. But he played and looked at books the way he did on any other morning, then Mommy helped him get ready for school. After lunch he said goodbye and met Jim Parsloe at the corner. They walked with the other kids, past the neighbors' houses until they got to kindergarten. Mattie knew it wouldn't be a good idea to tell Mrs. Thompson. When she made the class practice making letters, and later when he drew a picture of a horse eating grass, he did his work quietly and carefully.

During naptime, Janie Hutchins's dress got turned up and he could see her underpants. He almost laughed, but stopped himself in time. He closed his eyes and tried to rest. He felt a little proud because he didn't look again. Nothing much happened for the rest of that day. Jim said nothing much happened in the other class either. They walked home and punched each other a couple of times.

On Saturday, Mommy gave Mattie and his little sister Miriam ten cents each for the candy store. They could go by themselves since it was just across the baseball field. Mattie had to help Miriam climb the high wooden steps in front of the store. The heavy door always stuck, and had a part on the handle that you pressed down so it went clank. Inside, the store was smaller than Mattie's bedroom. He and Miriam stood and picked out what they wanted. The store smelled like bubble gum, red licorice, and something else dusty and old. Behind the candy counter there were things like cigarettes and magazines. Sometimes the candy store lady was nice. Other times she was mean. Mattie was afraid of her, but not as much as Miriam was. The other kids called the candy store lady Mary. Mommy said they should call her Mrs. Nitsky.

That day, Mrs. Nitsky smiled and waited while they made up their minds. The big round jars full of candy looked like goldfish bowls. Some kinds of candy were sparkly and colorful, others were smooth and dull, covered with a white dust. Mattie got three wax pop bottles, some peppermints, and some Tootsie Rolls. Miriam bought a chocolate bar and five Pixy Stix that Mattie knew he would have to help her with. He reached their dimes up to Mrs. Nitsky, who handed him two paper bags. He tried not to let the door slam when they left.

It was warm outside, so they sat on a bench beside the baseball field. Miriam dropped her chocolate bar in the dirt. While she cried and cried, Mattie brushed at it with his hand and then his sleeve, but the dirt wouldn't come off. Then the chocolate started to melt. The more Mattie tried to get the dirt off, the louder Miriam cried. Finally he gave her one of his pop bottles. She bit off the wax end and swallowed it, then sucked out the juice with little slurpy noises. The pop bottles were Mattie's favorite, but he didn't mind letting his sister have one. Jesus was happy that he gave Miriam one of his pop bottles.

Every day Mattie did his best in kindergarten, and his afternoons were mostly fun. When Mrs. Thompson said everyone could bring one favorite toy to school, he brought the little astronaut men he got for his birthday. For a long time none of the other kids wanted to play with them, until one day Mattie and three other boys played astronauts against cowboys, and the whole class gathered around to watch. On another day they cut black cats out of construction paper, and decorated them for Halloween. Mattie made big purple glittery eyes for his cat, and gave it long orange pipe-cleaner whiskers. Mrs. Thompson helped him tape the tail back on when it accidentally came off.

Mattie and Jim were walking home from school one day when a big girl ran past them, crying. "The president got shot in the head and killed!" she screamed. Mattie and Jim looked at each other. They couldn't believe a big girl had talked to them. When Mattie got home, Mommy was quiet and serious. She told him the same thing the big girl said. The president was shot. He died. Matty thought Mommy might give him a hug, but she didn't do anything different, or say anything else about the president. She went into the kitchen and started peeling potatoes for supper. Mattie watched her from the doorway for a minute.

"Did the president ask Jesus to come into his heart?" he asked.

She looked sad for a minute and then shook her head. "I don't think so. Go upstairs and play now, Mattie."

The next day, Jim told Mattie that at his house the TV was on all the time now, but not for their usual shows. His mom and dad didn't want to talk about anything but the president. They even ate in front of the TV, and Jim's mom cried a lot while they watched. Mattie didn't say anything. After Mommy talked to him that one time, no one at his house said anything else about the president. They didn't watch the news about it on TV. Mommy and Daddy were a little bit quiet, but they let Miriam run around making noise the same as usual. No one seemed very sad. But Jim and everyone else Mattie knew talked all the time about the man who shot the president and about the funeral and the brave little boy. Mattie couldn't understand it. He felt different from other people. Why weren't his mommy and daddy sad?

As he got older, Mattie got used to being different. Or at least he got used to knowing he was different. It was hard to get used to the feeling. And it took a long time to figure out why he was different.

Sometimes he thought it was his dad's job. "Your friends' dads make steel," his mom told him once. "Your dad sells it." Mattie wasn't sure which was better. His dad went to work in a coat and tie. Jim's dad came home from work in gray pants and a gray shirt, with his fingernails black around the edges. Sometimes Jim's dad talked loud and seemed scary, but other times he kidded with Mattie and made him laugh. When Jim was at Mattie's house, Mattie's dad didn't talk to Jim at all. At Jim's house everyone watched TV and talked about sports and sang songs from the radio. Mattie never knew the songs, and he started watching TV at Jim's house so he could see more shows. Jim's dad liked to read westerns, but those were the only books Mattie saw at Jim's house. It seemed like Mattie's house was full of books, spilling out of shelves in every room.

Sometimes he stood on the family room sofa to look at the books lined up on the wall, while the TV behind him sat quiet until the right shows came on. There were books of sermons, and sets of books that all looked the same and were called commentaries, zigzagging down the shelves like the paths on a game board. Other sets with "systematic theology" in the titles contained thick books by Calvin, Edwards, Spurgeon, Hodge, Buswell, Vos, Machen. Mattie learned the names without thinking, just like he knew the flowers and berries on the wallpaper. He heard his mom and dad mention these names sometimes, so he thought they must have read the books once, maybe a long time ago before he and Miriam were born. He didn't see them reading them now.

Mainly it seemed like his mom and dad went to meetings. That was what they did instead of watching TV, or talking about sports, or listening to the radio. On Wednesday nights both his mom and dad went to prayer meeting, either at church or at someone's house. They took Mattie and Miriam along, and told them to read books or color pictures. Other meetings were for church committees that his mom and dad were on. Those could be two or three nights a week. Sometimes his dad or mom came home from a meeting and no one said anything about it. The evening continued the same as usual. Other times they talked for a long time afterward, and Mattie heard the names of people his mom and dad disagreed with, who were making trouble in the church. These were grownup talks that went past Mattie's bedtime. Sometimes he heard his mom cry. His dad's voice might get loud.

Mattie began to understand that it wasn't his dad's job that made them different. It had to do with church. Most of Mattie's friends went to church, but that wasn't the same. Their churches weren't like the ones where Mattie's family went. Other people went to church, but they didn't always believe for real, in their heart. You could go to church but not really be a Christian. At the churches where Mattie's family went, you could tell that most people were Christians. For one thing, they didn't smoke or drink. Mostly, though, you could tell because they thought about Jesus a lot and talked about him during the week. They read the Bible. They prayed before they ate. They said things like "Lord willing" and "Before I was saved."

Mattie heard his parents and people from church use a lot of these special expressions. People were Christians if they "knew the Lord." They called Jesus their "personal savior." They tried to have a steady "walk with the Lord" and not be "out of fellowship." They "spent time in the Word," usually in their daily "quiet time" when they would "lift up" their friends in prayer. When they decided to do something they said they felt "called" or "led," and instead of a safe trip they wished each other "traveling mercies." If they talked about sins they'd committed, they said they felt "convicted."

After a while Mattie noticed when people *didn't* talk this way. It was like going to school with your zipper down. He knew he wasn't supposed to judge others, but he couldn't help feeling better about someone who said "God's blessings to you" than about someone who said "Good luck." Sometimes he heard people joke about these church sayings, laughing at how they used them all the time without thinking. But they always used them anyway.

On Sunday mornings, Mattie, Miriam, and their parents all went to Sunday school, and then upstairs to church. At the end of the day, while it was still light in the summer, they went to the evening service while other kids played baseball or watched Walt Disney. Church was hard, especially the sermon. When Mattie started first grade his grandmother gave him a watch, so he knew that the sermon sometimes lasted an hour. There was also the long time standing up while the pastor prayed. Sunday school should have been easier, since it was meant for kids, but Mattie didn't always like it. He kept that a secret. He never told his mom or anyone else. By the time he was seven he knew all the Bible stories, and he got tired of singing "This Little Light of Mine" and "The Wise Man Built His House Upon a Rock" over and over again. A lot of the kids at church were boring, or annoying, or just no fun. When he went to school on Monday he was glad to be back with his real friends, like changing into comfortable old clothes. This was another secret feeling.

But then there were the times when he knew he believed. Once when he was in kindergarten the pastor came on a special morning and talked to all the Sunday school kids together. Instead of standing far away at the front of the church, high up in his preaching place, the pastor sat close to them on a little chair. The morning light made the air and the floor look yellow. Everyone's head turned cloudy and golden around the edges. The pastor talked about how much God loved them, and how he would always take care of them no matter what happened. Mattie never forgot the golden light and the pastor's serious, friendly eyes. During the church service, some hymns made Mattie feel so happy that he heard them in his head all through the week. His favorites were "This Is My Father's World" and "Fairest Lord Jesus." When he sang them he felt peaceful and glad to be a Christian. Everything fit together the right way deep inside him. He knew it wasn't only the words or only the tune. The words and music together filled him with love for God. Sometimes he almost cried.

For one week during the summer, beginning when he was ten, he and the kids from his church went to a camp called Maple Glen. It wasn't a "church camp" like where some of his friends from school went, but a "Bible camp." Maple Glen had been an old farm until a few years before Mattie started going there, and it always felt like it wasn't done being turned into a camp yet. A big dusty house stood beside a tree-lined lake, with a tire swing hanging over the brown water. Old pews and other church furniture cluttered the house, where meals and Bible classes were held, and where the girls slept upstairs. The boys slept in the chicken coop up the hill. Chapel meetings, where people sang hymns and Christian camp songs and accepted Christ as their savior, happened in the barn.

Mattie loved Maple Glen. At the church camps where his friends went, they played sports and made crafts and swam, all according to a daily schedule. Everyone knew exactly what came next. At Maple Glen, the teachers and counselors seemed to make up camp as they went along. There were Bible classes in the morning, and chapel after supper, but the rest of the time just flowed by itself. Instead of following a schedule, kids spent hours playing four-square on the shady patio, or swimming in the lake. If he felt tired, Mattie took a nap on his bunk or wrote a letter to his mom and dad. One of the main activities each day was throwing a counselor in the lake. With the cool dewy mornings and then swimming every afternoon, Mattie could never manage to keep his clothes dry, so when he got home his mom unpacked his suitcase and explained to him what mildew was.

Every night at the end of the chapel service, there would be an invitation. All the campers bowed their heads, and the speaker asked people to raise their hands if they wanted to accept Christ. The speaker always waited a long time, until he saw some hands. "Yes, I see that hand," he would say. "Praise God." Mattie had a hard time then, staring down at his sneakers on the concrete floor. He knew he had accepted Jesus that morning at the top of the stairs, but maybe, being so little, he hadn't understood. The speakers said that sometimes people thought they were Christians and were saved, but really they were just trying to act the right way and fit in at church. They didn't truly believe in their hearts. Mattie wanted to know for sure that he was saved. Some nights he almost raised his hand. But he never did, because he remembered that he prayed the way his mom had told him. It felt like Jesus came into his heart. He was pretty sure it still felt real.

On the last night of camp the counselors built a big fire in a meadow. Everyone sat around the fire, and a lot of kids stood up to give their testimonies. Some said they accepted Christ during the week. A lot more said they re-dedicated their lives to Christ. They said that the year before, at camp, they grew a lot in their faith, but then they backslid at school when they were around kids who didn't know the Lord. Now they wanted to follow Christ again. They were re-dedicating their lives to him. One of the counselors played a guitar, and everyone sang "Pass It On" or some other campfire song.

Mattie never stood up at the campfire, just as he never raised his hand in chapel. Whenever he thought about re-dedicating his life, he decided that his life was already dedicated. If he stood up and said he was re-dedicating his life, it would be almost as much a fake as if he pretended to be a Christian but didn't really believe. So he thought he was doing the right thing when he didn't stand up at the campfire, but he still felt uncomfortable. He didn't know for sure what he believed in his heart, or what he should do.

He met Kathy Baron his first year at Maple Glen. They liked each other right away. She was pretty, but in an ordinary enough way that Mattie didn't worry about competition from other boys. She had curly light-brown hair and a quick, easy way of moving that made him think she was probably better at sports than he was. He never tried to show off for her, playing basketball or softball. Instead they teased each other, waiting in the long line to play four-square. They exchanged glances in the noisy dining room, their eyes meeting across the jumble of heads and arms, and wobbling pitchers of bug juice. She laughed whatever he did, so he kept doing whatever would make her smile, whether it was making a funny face or imitating one of the counselors. They didn't sit together in chapel, or hold hands for three or four seconds when they hoped no one was looking. Only a few of the oldest kids did that. Mattie and Kathy just knew they liked each other. They didn't need to say it.

Mattie always knew that if he ever had a girlfriend she would have to be a Christian. When he was eight or nine he used to wonder about that, how he could like any of the girls he knew from church. A long time ago he was in love with a girl in Sunday school, whose name he didn't know and who had long straight brown hair and mischievous dark eyes. He never knew if she moved away or her family stopped coming, and ever since then the girls at church all seemed plain and boring. But Kathy from Bible camp was fun. In his bunk at night he imagined what it would be like if she moved to his town, or if their churches started doing barbecues or games together during the year.

On going-home Saturday that first summer, they stood near each other in the crowd of kids, surrounded by piles of suitcases and sleeping bags. Mattie tried hard to think of something to say. He couldn't ask for her address. It would be like asking her to marry him. Suddenly he saw his mom and dad get out of their car and start toward the milling campers. Without thinking, he reached over and touched Kathy's shoulder. She turned instantly, as if she'd been waiting. Her eyes grew wide and sad. She expected him to say something, but everything he thought of saying seemed wrong. He gave a little smile, and shrugged and waved. She waved back. Then his mom's pillowy arms were around him.

Despite his hopes for a massive church youth gathering, or that her family might visit his town for some reason and he'd happen to meet her on the street, he didn't see Kathy during the year that followed. He kept thinking he saw her in a store, or in a passing car, knowing he was just imagining things. He began to have trouble remembering her face. She became a voice that floated on the breeze or rang out across the crowded dining room. In the end he simply lived through the long dull months, going to school, watching TV, playing football and basketball with friends, until finally he didn't think about her very often.

And then it was time to go back to Maple Glen. To his surprise, he found himself looking forward to goofing off in the chicken coop and jumping off the tire swing, but not so much to seeing Kathy. After his parents had dropped him off, and he'd gotten through registration and taken his things up to the coop, he joined a group of kids on the patio, and there she was. As soon as she noticed him she gave him a big hug. He was shocked until he saw some other kids hugging each other, and remembered that people did that now, they hugged friends they hadn't seen in a while. So that was all it was. It didn't mean anything.

"It's so great to see you again, Mattie!"

"People call me Matt now."

"Oh. Sorry!"

He looked at her, taking in her appearance after so much time. She seemed different. How could someone change so much in a year? His first horrified impression was that she'd gotten fat, but he soon realized he'd been mistaken. She just looked less like a stringy kid. She didn't yet look like the junior high girls from church, but she definitely looked older. He would get used to her, he decided. It would be okay.

They still didn't sit together in chapel, but Matt found more chances for them to talk. He noticed that Kathy made herself easy to find. Standing on the muddy lakeshore, or joining the mass of kids drifting in to dinner, they exchanged bits of news and asked each other questions, picking up wherever they'd left off.

"I think you'd be a really *good* artist," she said in the four-square line.

"How come?"

"You have a good eye. Remember you saw that owl before anyone else?"

"And I spotted *you* right away," he dared to say. "Last year."

They abruptly turned to watch the players. The ball bounced with a hollow ringing sound beneath the patio roof. T-shirts and swimsuits glimmered in the shade. Jermaine, the one Black kid at camp, spiked the ball to claim the first square. Kathy jumped and caught it before it could roll into the lake.

One night after chapel, when it had gotten dark, the counselors staged a "Haunted Forest." Lanterns and flashlights lit gory scenes for the shuffling line of campers. Mangled figures slumped in seas of fake blood. Heads and limbs strewed the ground like fallen fruit. From deep in the woods came drawn-out howls and moans. Behind Matt, Kathy hooked her fingers into his belt loops and stayed close. Sometimes after a piercing scream her arms circled his waist. Matt put his hands over hers.

In the afternoons they split a bag of M&Ms from the snack bar, lounging in musty-smelling chairs beside the fireplace. The other kids had quit bothering to stare. Up in the coop Matt heard a crack or two from the guys, but he ignored them. He wasn't embarrassed, not even especially proud. Spending time with Kathy just seemed right. He didn't think about her constantly. He did the things he'd always liked doing at Maple Glen, and when he thought it would be nice to have her company she would usually be there. A few times one of them looked for the other, and once Matt even asked someone where she was. When they finally tracked each other down, he discovered her smile all over again.

On the last morning they did exchange addresses this time, scribbling on the back of a candy wrapper and carefully tearing it in half. They stood waiting, glum and silent. "Oh," Kathy groaned. "My parents." Then, quick as a minnow, she kissed him on the mouth. "Bye, Matt." She gathered her things and trotted toward the cars.

They wrote each other three or four times before Christmas. Matt snatched each letter from the pile of mail and hurried to his room to read it, but by the third one he had to admit to himself that the letters didn't interest him much. Kathy didn't seem to do a lot besides school. Her ordinary rounded handwriting left him lonely for the smiling girl by the lake. By March he couldn't remember which of them had let the correspondence drop. He thought she probably felt the same way. He never forgot her fingers tugging his belt loops, the sun in her eyes and on her slicked-back hair, her kiss on the noisy crowded lawn.

During those years there was trouble in his family's church—something Matt felt sure would never happen in his friends' churches. Other people went to church and went home. They didn't even go every Sunday, and nothing would ever happen there that could bother them the rest of the week. But at Matt's family's church, disagreements led to tense discussions, which led to separate groups trying to control the congregation. On Sunday nights Matt listened to his parents analyze what had happened. He learned to avoid the mysterious knots of grownups who stood around whispering after a service. Eventually he knew who belonged to his parents' side, and who belonged to the other. He accepted all of this as another thing that made his family different. If you really believed, then differences in belief were bound to happen.

The only reason their church existed in the first place was that people stuck by their beliefs. For years, Matt's parents had driven twenty minutes—twice every Sunday, and once or more during the week—to attend a church they felt was right for them. They could have gone to several other churches in their town of Stanton, but none of those held to quite the right doctrines, or were affiliated with the right denomination. Then Matt's dad and some others got the idea of starting a new congregation closer to where they lived. It would save people the laborious trip over cornfields and hills, and it would also serve as a kind of missionary effort, bringing their kind of Christianity to a place that needed it. Even as a boy Matt could sense his parents' excitement as the idea took hold and more people got involved. They would found a church that did things the right way. Every part of it, from the pastor to the elders to an eventual building, would be the result of their prayers, discussions, and decisions. Nothing would happen carelessly or through flawed theology. The church would grow in the right direction from the very beginning.

For the rest of his life, Matt remembered the ordinary, modest people who joined together to found the new church. In his imagination they grew into monumental figures, faith heroes like the martyrs and missionaries in books. He didn't understand the doctrines they fought for so fiercely, any more than he could read his parents' old commentaries and sermon collections. Those details floated vaguely in the background, while he got to know their voices and their kind, caring faces. Perhaps, he thought later, he loved his parents' friends in spite of their theology. He was certain only that they surrounded him like an extended family.

Doug and Jane McKeon lived two or three miles from Matt's house. He rode his bike there on errands for his mother. The brick house commanded an enormous sloping yard containing a trailer where Mr. McKeon's mother lived. When Matt got off his bike, he'd find Mr. McKeon crisscrossing the lawn on an old riding mower, one hand raised in greeting. Old Mrs. McKeon emerged from her trailer with a plate of cookies. The McKeons' daughter Cindy was three years older than Matt—too young to babysit him and Miriam when they were little, too old for them to play with. But as a teenager she sat with them in the little screened porch, telling secrets and making up stories, while the grownups discussed church matters inside.

Mr. McKeon worked in a warehouse for a building supply company, looking after tall stacks of lumber and siding. Matt pictured him on a forklift that rattled and roared like his mower. He would give the other men dirty looks when they swore, and tend his construction materials with the same sober care that he used in church when preparing the Lord's Supper. He told Matt that he memorized Bible verses to help him get through the day.

Willard and Eunice Caldwell were the oldest couple in the church. They remembered when the original church in the country was new, a lonely outpost for a handful of families. The young pastor, fresh from seminary, preached long intellectual sermons while the farmers dozed and their wives frowned. Mr. Caldwell always laughed when he described those days, the skin near his eyes puckering into fragile folds. He wore rimless glasses and fuzzy cardigan sweaters, his woolen trousers ironed into a faultless crease. Seated next to him at Wednesday night prayer meeting, Mrs. Caldwell smiled and said nothing. Although everyone respected and even honored the Caldwells, and Mr. Caldwell would sigh at times and make a solemn pronouncement, neither ever served in any official position. To Matt they just seemed to stand for something treasured and fading.

Besides the McKeons and the Caldwells there was a tiny handful of other regulars, some with kids whom Matt got to know better than he would have liked and some who showed up on Sunday mornings and went home without anyone getting to know them very well. Matt couldn't understand why those people came at all, why they would put up with such a different, demanding sort of place when they could go to any number of comfortable, well-established churches where no one bothered anyone else. After two or three years the little group approached the size of a congregation, gathering first in a township fire hall and then in a weather-beaten grange, where behind a stage with a velvet curtain there were tunnel-like passages for kids to explore while their parents sought God's will for the next building. In all the countless services he attended as a boy during those years, Matt couldn't remember once sitting in a pew. The church bought a hundred folding steel chairs, with a decal on each backrest bearing the manufacturer's name. Leaning forward during the sermon, Matt tried to peel the decal off in one delicate piece, before it could chip or tear. After a few years hardly any decals remained.

Shortly after the fire hall time, the church called its first pastor. He was also the first pastor to make a lasting impression on Matt. The word "tragic" always came to mind when he tried to remember what Gunther Hohenselig was like. It had something to do with the glistening black hair, the massive bluish jowls, the troubled, almost panic-stricken eyes. His voice, always broken and halting, caught painfully when his sermons reached an emotional climax. He never appeared in anything but a black or dark-blue suit, and Matt never once heard him laugh.

What everyone remembered about Pastor Hohenselig's time at the church was the sermon series he preached midway through his first year. Almost every sermon that Matt had ever heard started out with careful analysis of a Bible passage, but he couldn't remember a text that this series was based on. Instead he recalled the bleakness of the first three installments, set forth as if directly from the preacher's own convictions. "What does life really amount to?" Pastor Hohenselig asked, beginning the first sermon. He gazed sadly at his listeners, letting his question sink in. A person was born, went to school, got a job, got married. Children came along. Family routines were established. At some point life turned tedious and dull. A sameness set in. Hoping for some kind of spark, the person tried new adventures and hobbies, bought new things, found a different set of friends. Relief came for a while, but nothing really changed. Existence followed the same rut of feverish, meaningless activity. Every path ran up against the same blank wall.

By this point the congregation was shifting uncomfortably, waiting for the hopeful conclusion. It never came. "Is that all there is?" Pastor Hohenselig cried. "Is that all there is?" he repeated, his voice breaking. That was how the first sermon ended.

The second sermon offered more of the same, and the third dwelt even more starkly on the waste and futility of life. In all three sermons, Pastor Hohenselig preached with a passion no one had heard from him before. He'd found his message, his unmistakable theme. Finally, on the fourth Sunday, he spoke of joy and purpose in following Christ—but it was too late. The congregation had looked deep into Pastor Hohenselig's heart. No one believed in the happy ending. Again and again during the year that followed, Matt's parents discussed the problem of Gunther. The McKeons came over frequently, or Matt and Miriam played Monopoly with Cindy in the McKeons' screen porch while the grownups talked for hours. Matt never knew exactly how it came about that Pastor Hohenselig left. He remembered only the months of tension and frustration, and then the sad relief.

Not surprisingly, their next pastor was different in every way from Gunther Hohenselig—slightly built and good-natured, with a pleasant smile and a calm, soothing voice. Ten years younger than Pastor Hohenselig, Gerald Nash guided the church with a quiet humility, as if he would never dream of telling the elders what to do. Eventually Pastor Nash helped plunge the church into a graver crisis than the one created by Gunther Hohenselig, but Matt barely noticed, for it was Pastor Nash who baptized him, and with baptism came his first time taking communion.

In the years since he'd knelt at the top of the stairs, Matt had experienced many periods of doubt. He didn't doubt God, or the Bible, or the way to be saved. To all of that he still firmly adhered. He doubted himself. Was his faith sincere? Did he truly believe? Or was he one of those people whom adults always warned him about, who thought they were Christians but had never taken the decisive step? Once when he and his mother were arguing about something she thought he'd done wrong, she hesitated, then murmured, "Sometimes I wonder if you're a Christian at all." For weeks Matt was plunged into despair. What had made her say a thing like that? How often was "sometimes"? Surely his mother, who knew him better than anyone, saw into his heart and perceived his deepest thoughts. Even though she'd spoken partly in anger, she must have had some reason for questioning his faith. Maybe some part of him was holding back. Maybe he hadn't yet surrendered himself fully to the Lord.

When he managed to keep such doubts at bay, he got along happily enough. He found ways to balance faith and everyday life, church and school, being a good Christian and being a normal kid. "Normal" meant honest and real, with nothing fake or put on. In some essential part of himself, he wanted his faith to fit the life he actually knew. As an eight- or nine-year-old, he'd read a series of books about the "Bitter Gulch Boys," a bunch of kids his age who roamed a hilly wooded area much like his own part of western Pennsylvania. The gang's adventures always culminated in a rousing fistfight with a rival gang, and with some sinful wretch getting saved. Long after he'd outgrown the formulaic stories, Matt retained a deep-rooted belief that he could be a Christian and still hold his own in the world, at times with a well-placed punch in the nose.

At school, he avoided not only the kids from church but other brainy, straight-arrow types like himself. Especially in junior high and high school,

14

his friends tended to be oddballs who ate lunch together for no particular reason other than that they weren't popular kids, brains, or jocks. Some of them made Matt laugh, or he liked the creative expressions they used. One guy filled his school-issued writing tablets with caricatures and cartoons, as good as anything in the newspaper. Another could turn a few scraps of leather into a pair of beaded moccasins. Matt's friend Mike Hargrove, after one year of lessons, could play guitar like Eric Clapton. When the group got older they swore and partied and got into trouble. A few of them used drugs. But they always accepted Matt as the religious guy who didn't do any of that stuff. He didn't feel especially close to these friends, but he liked them. It felt right to him, being a Christian and being one of them. He felt normal.

He'd just begun figuring out this path through school when he turned twelve and it was time to be baptized by Pastor Nash, and examined by the elders before taking communion. All his doubts boiled to the surface. What if school and his friends were what really mattered to him, while at church he just put on an act? Wasn't that the sort of fraud his mom had accused him of being? Wasn't that what the chapel speakers always warned about at camp—that somehow, through years and years of being a good church kid, you could fool everyone as a pretend believer, and fail to make a true "decision for Christ"?

He met the elders in the pastor's study after a Sunday morning service. By this time the congregation had built a real church: a plain, steepleless brick structure on an acre of rocks and weeds that would someday become a lawn. Stuck into the rocks, a white-painted wooden sign said "Holy Savior Presbyterian Church. Gerald Nash, Pastor." The bare sanctuary contained the same steel folding chairs that the congregation had used in the fire hall and the grange. Nothing hung on the walls. The windows were tinted a solid amber. Some people had wanted to hang a shiny cross behind the pulpit, but Matt's father and others thought it would be too distracting. To worship God you needed nothing more than a simple room, the Word, and other believers.

Six chairs were carried into the pastor's study for Matt's meeting with the elders. Pastor Nash sat at his desk, facing Matt from the far end of the narrow room. Matt knew the five men who would question him, but he only knew Doc Hodges well. He'd been taken to the Hodges place—the doctor's office jutted out from the family home—for shots and checkups as long as he could remember. Once when Matt fell on a jagged tree limb, the doctor stared at his forearm for a minute or two and then closed the gash with a half-dozen stitches. Dr. Hodges rarely said anything except what was wrong with you and what he intended to do about it, but Matt trusted him and felt at home with him. The other elders were close to his father's age—mysteriously, his father never became an elder—and like his father they looked like they probably spent their free time reading books about theology. As Matt entered the study the men greeted him with solemn nods.

The first part was easy. Pastor Nash asked him to explain what he believed, and Matt recited the doctrines he'd heard all his life. When Pastor Nash smiled and made a note in a book, Matt swallowed and said, "But . . ." Everyone turned to look at him. Pastor Nash continued smiling. "Sometimes I don't know if I'm sincere," said Matt. The words sounded foolish, but he didn't know what else to say.

"I understand, Matt," the pastor said. "Our faith will probably never burn with a fire like David's or Paul's. But God accepts our simple, genuine trust."

"That's the problem," said Matt. "I'm not sure if my faith is genuine."

"Well," said Mr. Fotherington, a stubby man with gnarled hands and a raspy voice, "if you didn't genuinely believe, you wouldn't have put all of us to the trouble of being here, would you?"

"I don't know," said Matt. He suddenly wondered what he'd gotten himself into. He didn't even know how he wanted this to end. Maybe there was some kind of course for confused believers that he should take. "Sometimes," he said, "I think maybe I just do things to please my parents."

There was silence for several seconds. Everyone looked at the floor. Pastor Nash made another note in the book, while light from the window cast a shadow from his pen.

Doc Hodges re-crossed his legs and looked at Matt. Matt stared back at him, wishing he could leave.

"Matt," said Doc, "when you come see me and I prescribe some medicine, and your mother buys it and gives it to you, how do you feel about that medicine?"

"I don't feel anything about it," said Matt. "I just take it."

"Do you believe it will work?"

"I guess so. Yeah."

"Do you wonder if you believe sincerely that it will work?"

A few of the elders chuckled. Matt didn't say anything.

Doc Hodges gave him his gentlest smile. "They call Jesus the Great Physician. I'm confident he's *your* physician, Matt. I don't think you have anything to worry about."

The other elders relaxed back into their chairs. Pastor Nash beamed. A few more things were said, the pastor handed him a certificate, and Matt left the study to rejoin his parents. The following Sunday he stood at the front of the church while Pastor Nash asked him some questions and then, from a small bowl he held in his hand, sprinkled water on Matt's head. Matt didn't know what he should be thinking, or if he should say an inward prayer. The water pooled for a second on the top of his head, then seeped down into his hair.

He took communion two weeks later. Matt's Catholic friends talked about "First Communion," but no one at his church used that expression. When the day arrived he didn't wear special clothes, and he certainly didn't receive any presents, like his friends who got checks and twenty-dollar bills. Matt received communion with so little fuss that hardly anyone would have noticed. Yet everything—Pastor Nash's somber voice, the expressionless elders who removed and replaced the white cloths, the doleful hymns, the sad faces of the congregation—made Matt feel like he was joining in a moment of gravity and peril. Why else would they do it only four or five times a year? Pastor Nash read the verse from 1 Corinthians about the person who eats and drinks unworthily, and "eateth and drinketh damnation to himself." In other words, one false move and he was a goner. The trays of bread and cups of grape juice came down the row toward him, passing from hand to hand. He felt his mother watching as he took a bread cube and cupped it in his sweaty palm. He waited for Pastor Nash to say, "Eat ye all of it." For years afterward, he thought the words meant he must consume every crumb.

Just as when he'd been baptized, he wondered what he should think about, how to act at this moment. He knew the bread and grape juice were in remembrance of Christ, so he thought about the Last Supper, the trial and scourging, the crucifixion, the taunts, the vinegar, the two thieves, the last words, the soldier's spear. Had he forgotten anything? The bread trembled in his fingers. He closed them around the sticky morsel to make sure he wouldn't drop it.

When the service was over, Mr. and Mrs. Caldwell walked over to where Matt and his family were standing. Matt saw with surprise that they wanted to talk with him, not his parents.

"Did you take communion today, Matt?" asked Mr. Caldwell.

Matt nodded.

Mr. Caldwell said nothing, just smiled and placed a hand on Matt's shoulder. Mrs. Caldwell smiled too. It meant more to Matt than a dozen checks.

The problems in the church began that winter. Several new families had started coming, and made themselves at home right away. Matt never got to know the kids because they went to the new Christian school. Matt's parents exchanged only casual greetings with the adults. As the church grew, new people showed up fairly often, but these newcomers stuck out because something was up between them and Pastor Nash. Matt could tell. The new couples and the pastor stood talking together after services, and at basement potlucks they shared a table. After one dinner the people at that table sang a hymn or song that Matt had never heard before. His parents frowned down at their plates, then talked more loudly with the people at their own table. Matt got up to get more dessert.

As he returned, the refrain filled every corner of the basement: "And drink the best wine in the hall of the King, and drink the best wine with the King!" Matt didn't know anyone who drank wine. As the singing got louder—almost as if the singers really *had* been drinking a lot of wine—it sounded to Matt like a challenge, almost a taunt. At his family's table, his parents got to their feet and told Miriam to hurry up with her cake. Other people were leaving, too. His mother took his wrist and pulled him toward the stairs. He set his plate down and wrapped his cookies in a napkin.

On the drive home and for an hour afterward, his parents discussed the potluck. Matt hid behind the newspaper. It was going too far, his father said. They were dividing the church. It was almost as if they were *trying* to make everyone else leave. After each accusation, Matt's mother told his father to stay calm. No one could say definitely what the new people were trying to do. Yes, they were different, but sometimes Christians just had to live with people who weren't like themselves. Maybe—Matt heard the timid hope in his mother's voice—maybe the new people would be the ones who realized that they didn't fit in. Maybe they would be the ones to leave. His father laughed a bitter laugh Matt hadn't heard before.

At about that time, Pastor Nash preached a series of sermons on the Letter to the Hebrews. Matt lost track of how many sermons there were. It just seemed he'd been hearing about Hebrews for as long as he could remember. None of the sermons made sense to him—a lot of talk about the high priest Melchizedek, and the importance of going to Christ "outside the camp." What camp? Outside to where? It all sounded mysterious and strange. Matt's parents talked more and more, late at night and over breakfast, about Pastor Nash and "the Melchizedek people." From what he could make out, Matt agreed with his parents, because the sermons made it sound like being a Christian made you different from everyone else. For one thing, you went to the Christian school, not the public schools where Matt had always gone. But then the sermons went further, into ideas that were the strangest and most troublesome of all. The sermons seemed to say you should be different from other *Christians*, and set yourself apart in special ways. Matt kept remembering the wine-drinking song. People like Matt's parents and their closest friends didn't drink. Everyone understood that when they went to each other's homes there would be no alcohol. But it seemed like the new people were above all that. For the Melchizedek people, ordinary rules didn't matter, whether they actually drank wine or just sang about it in their favorite song. Somehow they'd gone beyond the old ways. Matt never learned the details, but they had a different system of belief, and a different set of customs to go with it.

The day that Matt's father came home from a meeting and announced that the Melchizedek people were spreading a heresy, Matt knew the situation was getting serious. The phone rang a lot over the next few days. On several warm spring nights his father left the house abruptly, and returned looking as if he'd spent the last two hours arm-wrestling, and his features had frozen in a scowl.

When it had reached the point where no one could talk about anything but the troubles at the church, the McKeons invited Matt's whole family for dinner. Mrs. McKeon met them at the door, drying her hands on her apron, giving her hesitant smile that always looked as if she were about to cry. Her dark brown eyes curved down at the corners, and her lips drew back in a long straight line, showing the gaps between her teeth. Matt looked at her again. She *was* crying. Mr. McKeon stepped forward and put his arm around her. He said could you believe those Pirates were losing again, as Cindy came downstairs and everyone moved to the dining room. Matt smelled pot roast and mashed potatoes.

The McKeons never bothered with fancy preliminaries. When you arrived, you sat down to eat. Mr. McKeon reached toward Cindy and Matt on either side of him, and they all joined hands while he said grace. "In the precious name of Jesus," he concluded. "Amen," everyone said. In the same serious way that Matt imagined him doing his job at the warehouse, Mr. McKeon sliced the pot roast and handed it around. Matt's mom and Mrs. McKeon discussed biscuit recipes. The two fathers talked about work. Matt and Miriam and Cindy said nothing, just concentrated on Mrs. McKeon's delicious food. For dessert she brought out warm apple pie and home-made vanilla ice cream.

"How about a game of Monopoly?" Cindy asked Matt and Miriam as soon as dessert was over. Matt almost laughed, the suggestion sounded so coached. Miriam jumped up and followed Cindy to the porch. Matt stayed in his chair. His mother frowned across the table, her coffee spoon dinging against Mrs. McKeon's china.

Mr. McKeon's grin flashed in his big square head. He passed a hand over the gray bristles. "I don't see why Matt can't stay with us," he said. "He wants to know what's going on. I don't blame him."

Matt tried to look serious and grown up. Inside he was edgy with suspense. Matt's mother glanced at his father, who nodded slightly.

"Well, why don't we go into the living room," said Mrs. McKeon. With a thumping of chairs and a clatter of cups and saucers they re-settled in the next room, where Matt had been only once or twice. Unlike the McKeons' family room, where an afghan-strewn sofa faced a portable TV, and their retriever Henry had a smelly bed of old blankets, the living room looked meticulously tidy and formal. Framed photographs stood on the piano and end tables. Every surface not occupied by a picture frame seemed to hold a different translation of the Bible, or one of those Christian-lady novels that Matt's mom liked to read, or a book of devotions that had stuck in it a plastic bookmark with a knotted silk tassel. Matt sat in the corner beside the piano, on a plump chair that turned out to be harder than it looked.

The McKeons had asked his parents over because on the previous evening Mr. McKeon had attended a colloquium—he pronounced the unfamiliar word with distaste—at the church. The meeting had been mentioned in the church bulletin, but Matt's parents would never have gone. Similar meetings had been announced for several months, and everyone knew the Melchizedek people were behind them. Mr. McKeon had decided to go and find out what they were saying. He'd stayed until the end, he said, although what he heard made him angry and sad. No one spoke to him during the entire evening. It felt worse than if he'd been a stranger.

"Janice," Mr. McKeon said, looking gravely at Matt's mother. "Mark." He turned to Matt's dad. "I heard nothing like the Gospel that night. You wouldn't have recognized anything they were talking about. I looked at those four walls, built not so long ago to house the pure preaching of the Word, and I wondered how they had now come to harbor an entirely different gospel."

"It's heresy," said Matt's father. "I've been saying that."

"Well I sure couldn't make any sense of it," said Mr. McKeon. "That's what drove me wild. If it had been error plain and simple I would have been upset, but at least I would have known what I was dealing with. Instead it was all a bunch of gibberish. There was just one thing that someone said, that I can't get out of my mind."

He stopped to collect himself. Mrs. McKeon laid a hand on his knee.

"I don't know the fellow's name," said Mr. McKeon. "Maybe you would. You've seen him. Anyway, he was talking about our faith, the faith that all of us in this room confess, that we confessed long before those people came. And after a while he made a face and he said, 'All that stuff about the blood makes me sick.'"

In the silence Matt felt his breathing slow. He heard a big clock ticking in the hallway, and someone thumped a game piece across the Monopoly board. Resting his forearms on his knees, Mr. McKeon stared at Matt's parents. "He was talking about the blood of Jesus, that saves us from our sins," he said. His taut features reddened. He shook his head. "I don't know what we're going to do. I hardly know the place anymore."

"I know what you mean, Doug," said Matt's father. "I feel the same way."

Matt's mother sighed and squeezed her napkin into a ball. Mrs. McKeon began collecting cups and saucers. When she returned from the kitchen her husband said, "What do you say we bring all of this before the Lord? I can't think of anything else to do."

All four adults prayed. Matt noticed the calm, simple way they addressed God, almost as though they were thinking out loud. They recalled their years with the church, how they'd nurtured it from a daring, hopeful idea. They spoke of the pain the last few months had brought. They asked for wisdom and healing. Toward the end, faltering, Matt's father asked God to guide them if staying at Holy Savior Church became impossible. Beside him Matt heard his mother softly moan.

The Lindleys, the McKeons, and several other families left the church in the following weeks. Matt had thought their departure would be a dramatic event, with people from the church trying to persuade them to stay, and long, gloomy days and nights at home as the reality of what his family had done sank in. He'd imagined the shocked faces of Pastor Nash and others, maybe even an article in the local newspaper. But none of that happened. Matt's family just stopped going to Holy Savior. His parents quit attending meetings during the week, and gradually Matt stopped hearing the names of people who still went there. After a while it was as if they'd never known those people at all. Old church bulletins lying around the house disappeared. The list of phone numbers taped to the wall was replaced. Emptying the wastepaper baskets one Saturday morning, Matt found a crumpled record of their offerings to the church, written in his mother's round careful hand.

It seemed like a failure—but of what? Matt's parents had put so much time and energy—so much *love*—into a new local church that would embody their deepest beliefs, and now it seemed like nothing had been accomplished. Had they made a mistake somewhere? Were the Melchizedek people to blame for coming in and wrecking a good place? Or did churches just run their course and die sometimes? Matt waited for the family dinner conversation that would explain everything, and tie up the loose ends, but that too was just another satisfying, conclusive scene that never happened. Before long, the name "Holy Savior" was never mentioned in the house. Matt didn't notice a difference in his parents, but he reasoned that something permanent must have happened to them. If he felt sad and defeated, then they must feel a lot worse.

The families who left Holy Savior scattered to churches around the area. Some saw an opportunity to experiment a little, explore something new. For the Lindleys, however, where to go next was never in question. The Sunday after their last at Holy Savior, they returned to Ebenezer Bible Church, the congregation from which the founding families had begun. As they drove past fields and thickets they hadn't seen in years, Matt felt like they'd been exiled to the wilderness.

The people at Ebenezer knew what had happened, and felt bad for the Lindleys. But no one asked for details, or blamed the Melchizedek people, or commended Matt's family and the other exiles whom Matt's father liked to call "the faithful departed." It wasn't that their Ebenezer friends were being tactful. They just weren't interested. They cared about the Lindleys, and went out of their way to welcome them back and include them, but they simply had no appetite for controversy. In their small town in a quiet valley nothing ever changed, and they liked it that way. They knew who they were and they knew their place.

Ebenezer hadn't always shied away from conflict. The church began during the wars between fundamentalism and "modernism," when Ebenezer Bible Church refused to compromise with liberal theology, especially liberal ideas about the Bible. Every word of scripture was inspired by God, those first leaders had maintained, and its account of history was true, from Creation through the Second Coming, with no need for any modern analysis or interpretation. Fortunately for Matt, who found the old controversies embarrassing and not very important, that chapter of Ebenezer history had been nearly forgotten. The congregation might have forged its identity in an era of bitter schisms and doctrinal disputes, but those battles had been fought long ago. The current members took for granted their hard-won legacy of sound, safe teaching. Far from being grim warriors, the Ebenezer people whom Matt got to know cared mainly about Wednesday-night prayer meeting attendance, and making sure covered-dish dinners were organized in the proper manner.

Unlike Holy Savior, where Matt had had to admit to himself that he didn't much like the other kids, Ebenezer had almost no "brethren" his age to worry about. A few older kids remained from his family's first years there, but these were in the process of moving away. The congregation consisted of upper-middle-aged and older people, with three or four young families. When he began high school Matt was drafted to teach a Sunday school class, simply because no other teenagers were available. He told Bible stories to his handful of six-to-eight-year-olds, watching them coil like springs before bolting for the door. He found himself getting to know his parents' friends, although these relationships were nothing like the warm, intense closeness his family had had with the McKeons and others.

People from the surrounding Pennsylvania and Ohio counties referred to Ebenezer Bible Church as "Will Huffaker's church." Will had been the pastor there when Matt was small. Upon the Lindleys' return, he greeted them with the same descending three-note chuckle and bashful smile, the same wavy black hair turned mostly gray. He had a round nose and wide dark-brown eyes, and wore suits that looked a size too small. Everyone, even the kids, called Will by his first name, and razzed him the way they would any member of the congregation. Hardly anyone knew his wife Jean, whose infrequent presence at the church made it clear that she had plenty enough to do, taking care of her own four children.

Will possessed an impish side that came out when adults weren't around. Once at Maple Glen he'd refused to surrender the tire swing, requiring ten struggling boys to tumble him into the water. His cannonball-induced tidal waves were legendary. At covered-dish dinners he liked to snatch a piece of cake when Matt wasn't looking, then offer an innocent round-eyed stare. Seconds later Matt would discover his cake had been restored—usually a larger piece, with more frosting on it. As a teenager Matt got to see more of Will's clowning when he joined the church basketball team. In white shorts and a plain white T-shirt, Will dribbled at the top of the key before firing a no-look pass to someone under the basket. Or just when everyone expected him to pass, he would raise one knee and put up an old-fashioned two-handed set shot that almost always went in. When he made a shot he hollered "*Tell* my baby in Topeka!" or "*That's* a sweet cuppa joe!" There were people who claimed that one of his cross-over dribbles really did make a defender sprain his ankle. If someone swore during a game, whether an Ebenezer player or an opponent, Will would call out, "Keep it clean, boys, keep it clean." His face would redden any time he heard the Lord's name taken in vain.

When Will got into the pulpit, all such mischief disappeared. He wasn't mournful the way Pastor Hohenselig had been, but no one hearing him on Sunday mornings would suspect he'd ever laughed. A sweet smile of assurance might touch his lips when he described God's faithful care, but other than that he preached with stone-faced sobriety, stepping back now and then as if awed by a sudden revelation, raising a pudgy forefinger to emphasize an admonition. He never harangued his congregation, gripping the pulpit and raising his voice. That would have been assertive, and Will was never assertive. He stood upright and calm, letting the Gospel speak for itself.

Over the years, Matt realized that Will's sermons left out not just his mischievous self but any self whatsoever, any vestige of his own thoughts or feelings. He was deliberately and scrupulously unoriginal, for the simple reason that he wished to say nothing more than what the Bible said. He would have been appalled if someone had remarked that he'd brought his "personal perspective" to a passage of scripture. He regarded himself as a neutral conduit for the Word. His own personality could only distract from the power and purity of that Word.

Will's sermons always began with a theme—"The Assurance of Salvation," "Comfort in Affliction," "Resisting Temptation," "The Truth of the

Bible"—and a text. Instead of analyzing that text in detail, however, as Matt had heard—and would continue to hear—many preachers do, Will read the passage aloud to get himself going, then composed the bulk of the sermon from scripture that he drew on from memory. He didn't just stitch together brief sayings that everyone knew, like "The Lord is my shepherd" or "Pray without ceasing." He quoted whole passages, rolling out the stately King James cadences and peppering them with gestures and pauses. Now and then Matt tried to estimate the number of Will's own words in a sermon. They came to a pretty paltry total, compared to the pages of quoted scripture.

On one memorable occasion Matt did get to hear the pastor in his own words. Shortly after he'd received his driver's license, he asked his mother if he could take her car to the church for some Sunday school materials he needed. The trip to Ebenezer had been one of his most frequent practice routes, so she smiled and handed him the keys. With only a trace of nervousness, he set out over the familiar roads, steering carefully around the long tight curves, adjusting the gas to the slow climbs and steep descents. The trip felt longer when he made it by himself, but he got there without any problems.

It was a Saturday afternoon. He parked in the deserted lot and paused a moment. Compared to Holy Savior on its acre of dirt, Ebenezer boasted an ecclesiastical splendor. Its steeple reached as high as any of the neighboring houses. A stubby wing extended from the sanctuary, containing a tiny vestibule and space for coatracks. Except for Will's office, the space not used for worship was confined to the basement, where as a child Matt had attended Sunday school. Sprawling yew bushes surrounded the building, and flanked the steps that led up to heavy wooden doors.

Matt got out and entered the building. No lights were on, but a few cracks of sunshine parted the shadows. His sneakers squeaked in the Saturday stillness. He walked over glimmering tile past the hushed sanctuary, down a short hall to Will's office. He knocked on the open door.

Will looked up. He'd been writing on a pad like the ones Matt got at school. His worn black Bible lay open at his elbow. "Hello, Matt," he said, getting to his feet and stepping around the desk. "I have everything you need right here. Any questions?"

Matt took the sheaf of papers. "I don't think so," he said. "This should be fine." He hesitated. "But do you have a minute? To talk, I mean?"

Will looked at Matt for a moment, then closed the door. "Have a seat," he said, motioning toward two chairs in the corner.

"What's on your mind?" Will asked, sitting down across from Matt. In his flannel shirt and baggy khaki pants he looked ready to listen all afternoon.

As he was about to begin, Matt noticed a row of books on a shelf, leaning against a carton of paper plates and a baseball glove. There were several Bible translations, a Bible concordance, a Bible dictionary, and an atlas of the ancient world. There were no other books in the office, just the Bible on the desk. Matt couldn't help remembering his parents' sermons and commentaries zigzagging down the shelves. He looked back at Will's expectant face.

"I've been having some doubts," he said.

Will nodded. "Doubts about what?"

"Oh, not about God or the Bible or anything like that." Here he was, back being examined by the elders at Holy Savior, back with his same old problems. He almost wished he'd taken the Sunday school papers and left. "I guess I don't know if my faith is real. I say I believe everything we talk about here, but at school I'm the same person I always am. Sometimes I wonder if I really mean it."

Will's face expressed nothing. Matt knew that meant he was concentrating. "How long have you worried about this?"

Matt gave a short laugh. "Pretty much my whole life. You could say it comes and goes."

Will waited another few seconds, then said, "Matt, I think you want me to tell you whether you're really a Christian or not. Whether you're saved, as we'd say." He smiled.

Matt smiled back and waited.

"Well, my honest opinion on that question would be yes," said Will. "But I don't think you'd be satisfied with that. What you want is to be absolutely convinced on your own. That's why you can't quit worrying."

"Yes," said Matt, so quickly and fervently that they both laughed.

Will glanced at his desk, toward his open Bible, as if resisting the urge to pick it up. He pursed his lips and looked back at Matt.

"Scripture talks about God being our rock," he said. "'The Lord is my rock, and my fortress, and my deliverer,' says the psalmist. Growing up, you probably sang a hundred times about the wise man who builds his house upon a rock."

Matt nodded. "At least a hundred."

"Well, let's think about that rock. Picture a really big one. Big as your house, or bigger. That's what you're standing on. A huge, solid rock that's almost like a mountain. And that rock doesn't move."

"But . . ."

Will lifted a forefinger, as if he were in the pulpit. "I know. Sometimes our faith is weak. We might think we're putting on an act. We look at our lives and we feel like a bunch of phonies. Listen, Matt." Will fixed him with a stare. "Remember this. It's something that has helped me through some difficult times. Your legs might get shaky on the rock, but the rock never shakes."

Matt returned Will's gaze. Even if he'd disagreed, he wouldn't have challenged the authority in Will's voice, or the command that he take his words to heart. Then, suddenly, Will's face relaxed into a smile. "God bless you, Matt," he said. "Let's pray." After Will had said a few words, Matt stood up to leave.

At the door the pastor's voice stopped him. "Tell your mom her shoofly pie at the covered-dish dinner was delicious."

"Okay," said Matt. He glanced back one more time. Will sat at his desk, scribbling notes on his pad, one finger laid on his open Bible.

Driving home, Matt concentrated on the road again. It was October. The late sun flickered on dry stalks and pods, and flared in the reds and yellows of the trees. Like a faithful pony his mom's Reliant chugged up and down hills. He thought about the giant rock that never shakes. He remembered what Doc Hodges had said about medicine, how it didn't matter how sincerely you believed it would work. Something there, he told himself. Something to remember when he needed to get this feeling again.

He stopped at a neighborhood store to buy a gallon of milk. The girl at the cash register gave him a flirty smile. When he got home, his mother looked up from her book.

"Oh, you got some milk! That was thoughtful of you, Matt. I wondered what took you so long."

"Will and I were talking about your shoofly pie. He said it was delicious."

"Go on."

"He did."

In the years that followed the Lindleys' exodus from Holy Savior, Matt began high school and got more serious about his studies. He took electives in American and World History, pushing himself to do more research, analyze more closely, consider more complex problems. Will's sermons, with their simple messages and repeated Bible passages, seemed to belong to a different world, just as Harrington, the town where Ebenezer sat on an out-of-the-way corner, seemed a different world from the larger, busier Stanton. Matt listened to Will preach his standard sermon on the forgiveness of sins, quoting the same passages from Isaiah and Psalms, and the next day a problem in Algebra made him think harder than he'd ever thought in his life. After a Sunday morning service he turned to the people behind him, making small talk about the weather or his vague college plans, then with his school friends he debated music on the radio, compared opinions about girls and movies, and thought up ways to survive the conformity of marching band. From his courses he began to surmise that Christianity was more complicated than one of Will's three-point sermons—it better be, or what did it have to offer a complicated world?—and from spending time with his friends he found he had a lot in common with people who didn't go to Bible camp or Sunday school. He loved the congregation at Ebenezer, just as he'd loved Doug and Jane McKeon at Holy Savior; but the older he got the more he realized how much he needed honesty. He couldn't deny experiences that troubled his faith. When it came to understanding the world and himself, he wouldn't let his beliefs screen out what his eyes took in, and what his common sense told him was true.

One Saturday afternoon Matt sat in Mike Hargrove's basement, watching Mike play his electric guitar. It was like a free concert. Mike didn't get self-conscious, or try to show off. He just naturally played so well that Matt was enthralled. When they'd both had enough of the music, Mike put his guitar down and they ate beef jerky and talked. Mike's dad liked to hunt and fish, and bought beef jerky by the case. Chewing the tough meat in the dingy basement, with Mike's riffs and chords still echoing in their ears, they discussed all sorts of topics and never got bored. Matt got together with other friends to play basketball, or to swim or ride bikes, but they never talked the way he and Mike did. Only with Mike did Matt talk in any detail about his faith. With his other friends he was just "the religious one."

"What don't you like about them?" asked Mike, about a hard rock band that everyone was listening to at the time.

"The lyrics, mainly," Matt admitted. "I can't get into a band that tries to make Satan sound cool."

Mike laughed. "You always take things too seriously. They aren't Satanists, they just like to wear black and sing about spooky stuff. It's no different from slasher movies, really. Good clean fun."

"Uh huh," said Matt with a wry smile. "I guess it comes down to what you think is okay to fool around with. What they do just isn't my style."

"That's cool," said Mike. "Seriously, I can respect that."

In the last few months Mike had begun teasing his curly blond hair into a springy orb that gave him a sweetly angelic look. He used a pick, he'd explained to Matt, who thought at first that he meant a guitar pick. Seeing his mistake, Mike had strung him along, taking a pick from his guitar case and pretending to tidy up his hair. He still did it now and then, just to make Matt laugh.

"It's weird," said Matt. "People do songs about Satan and they're all over the radio, but the songs about Jesus never get played."

"Are they any good?"

"No."

They laughed.

"To tell the truth, the ones I've heard are pretty terrible," said Matt.

"There's 'Jesus Is Just Alright,'" said Mike.

"Yeah." It felt like Mike was trying to console him.

Mike got two more sticks of beef jerky from the box, and thoughtfully unwrapped his. "What is it with you and Jesus, anyway?" he asked. "Lots of people go to church, but with you it's like a major deal."

"Do I seem like a freak?"

"No, I don't mean anything like that. I wouldn't hang out with you then. You take it more seriously, though. It's a big part of you, not just a thing you do on Sunday morning."

"Yeah," Matt said, "that's supposed to be the idea. That's a compliment, really. I must be doing something right."

"What I want to know is, how come?"

"You mean why do I believe?"

"Why do you believe in that particular way, like a saved born-again person—no offense."

Matt smiled. "I'm not really sure. Maybe I'll figure that out someday."

Mike nodded. "You keep at it, man. And I'll keep trying to figure out the chords to 'Soul Survivor.'"

In the spring semester of his junior year, with some electives left to fill, Matt signed up for a course known as "Home Ec for Guys." On the first day the teacher addressed the class. "I know you're all here for an easy A," she said, throwing out a contemptuous smile. "And if you show up and try a little bit, that's exactly what you'll get." Matt looked around the kitchen at the rows of burners and the battered utensils on the walls. His classmates listened with dead expressions. He felt depressed and vaguely ashamed, but at least he might learn how to cook scrambled eggs.

That afternoon he had the second half of his American History survey with Mr. Donatello, the baseball coach. Matt had enjoyed the first half of the course, and done well. After Mr. Donatello got the class working on a personal statement about the meaning of history, he sat down at the empty desk in front of Matt. The coach had a perpetual tan, and a big mustache like Reggie Jackson. His polyester tie looked like it was made of plastic. He propped an elbow on Matt's desk and folded his hands in front of him. The class settled into a goofing-off hum. Mr. Donatello looked at Matt like he was a pitcher he couldn't figure out.

"What else are you taking this semester?" he asked.

Matt told him. When he got to the home ec course he mumbled a little. Mr. Donatello scowled and shook his head.

"What do you want to take a crap course like that for?"

Matt shrugged. "It seemed like it might be useful someday."

"You should take my course on social problems."

"I should?"

"Yeah. You're good at this sort of thing."

"But the semester's already started."

Mr. Donatello lifted his eyes to the buzzing lights. "Don't give me that. Drop the other one. Add this one. Take you fifteen minutes."

Matt asked Mr. Donatello what the social problems course was like. The coach described it, and it sounded interesting. Then Matt thought about never having to see the institutional kitchen again. He smiled at Mr. Donatello, who gave a small smile back.

"Okay," said Matt.

Mr. Donatello wasn't the best teacher Matt ever had, but Social Problems became his favorite course that semester. He read books about segregation, drug addiction, and poverty. He started reading more than sports and comics in the newspaper. For his "hands-on" project, he volunteered at a food pantry that was run by a big liberal church downtown. His mother lent him her car keys with tight lips and averted eyes. His final paper analyzed safety regulations at the local steel mill. Returning the graded paper, Mr. Donatello lingered by Matt's desk. His mustache looked fierce.

"You need to keep doing this kind of thing," he said, tapping the paper. "You know that, right?"

"I'm thinking about it," said Matt. When he had a chance to look at his grade he read beneath the circled A, in Mr. Donatello's jagged handwriting, "Shows real talent and conviction. A well-researched, inspiring piece of work."

Social Problems made it a memorable spring, but an even more consequential event took place later that semester, when Matt's gym class began the wrestling unit. Each year he dreaded the six weeks on the mat, and each year seemed worse than the one before. The brawniest, most competitive guys loved the wrestling unit, while the rest of the class endured it, waiting to take up track and softball outside. Matt especially hated wrestling in front of the class, when Mr. Phillips chose two opponents who would face off by themselves. It was supposed to be a kind of final exam, when the wrestlers would employ the moves Mr. Phillips had taught them; but the matches always went to the usual gym class heroes, who used brute force and spur-of-the-moment tactics to dominate people like Matt. Mr. Phillips heaped praise on the victors, pretending he'd taught them everything they knew.

On the third day of matches Matt still hadn't been called on. He knew his turn must be due. He sat with the others around the big blue mat, preparing to get it over with. He was wearing his best gym shorts, which gave his confidence a boost, and he felt good, in a hopeful mood, a little more relaxed than usual. He would give this unavoidable test his best effort, and see what happened. Mr. Phillips called his name for the third match of the day. His opponent was Ben Cameron.

Cameron's family had moved into the school district the year before. Since Seneca High was fairly small, he was still considered a new kid. He'd formed a circle of friends, but Matt hadn't picked up more than his name and a general impression from seeing him around—the sort of rough idea you formed about anyone in school, but in Cameron's case a bit sketchier because he was new, as well as being reserved. He seemed quiet in a confident, "Don't mess with me" kind of way. He didn't try to intimidate people, but he didn't exactly put them at ease, either. After Mr. Phillips called their names for the match, Matt and Cameron stood up and walked to the center of the mat, where they took their stances and awaited the signal.

Cameron wore his straight brown hair parted in the middle, and always kept his eyes slightly narrowed. He had a long bony face and a lean bony frame. In a low crouch, hands raised, fingers twitching, he trained his eyes on Matt's midsection. Matt did the same, as if playing defense in basketball. When the whistle blew, Matt leaned forward, bouncing on his toes, looking for an opening. He felt Cameron grab his leg, and the next thing he knew he was lying on his back. Cameron's face hung above him like a surgeon's.

Matt flipped onto his stomach, barely avoiding the instant pin. Cameron had him by both legs now. Matt worked himself into a seated position, wrapped his arms around Cameron's back, and held on. He had no plan except to last a while, and then maybe to last a while longer. He'd take it a few seconds at a time. His abdominal muscles strained painfully, as if he'd done fifty sit-ups. From far away, mingling with the roaring in his ears, he heard the class yelling his name. His arms began to slip. Just when he was about to end up on his back again, immobilized by Cameron's wiry arms and heavy chest, he slithered onto his side, got some traction, and heaved to his feet. Cameron's grip fell away. They stood in their original crouches, a small smile playing on Cameron's lips.

Before Matt could think about what to do next, Cameron dove for his legs, but this time he was ready and leaped backwards, at the same time throwing himself over Cameron's back. Each kept his footing, sidestepping and tiptoeing across the mat. For a few seconds they revolved, locked in a tense dancing arch. Then Matt must have stepped too close. Cameron had him by the leg again. They hit the mat hard, Matt twisting to avoid landing on his back. He sat rigid while Cameron, behind his right shoulder, tried to work him around and down for the pin. Matt planted himself, too exhausted to do more than hold on.

Cameron's grip around his waist seemed to ease a little, so he tried to scrabble up and get his feet under him. He made it halfway. Forced onto his side, he felt Cameron change positions and press his full weight down, lowering Matt's shoulder blades. It didn't take long then. Mr. Phillips's hand slammed the mat.

Cameron sprang up and returned to his place. Matt got slowly to his feet. "Wow, Lindley," said Mr. Phillips. "Good job."

In the locker room guys kept talking about the match. Matt couldn't figure out why until someone told him that Ben Cameron was on the wrestling team, a star in his weight class. He'd won two matches at the state tournament. The information helped explain Cameron's obvious superiority, but left Matt more puzzled than ever by his own performance. How had he held out so long? Looking back on those blurry few minutes, he could hardly recognize himself. On his way out of the locker room he came upon Cameron hoisting an enormous gym bag, about to leave for his next class. Matt stopped.

"That was great," he said. "You were, I mean. Thanks for not making me look too bad."

Cameron broke into a smile and shook Matt's hand the jock way, thumbs up. "You did good, man. You want to get lower, though." He put the gym bag down and demonstrated, assuming the familiar crouch. "Always lower."

"Ah. Well . . . have a good season."

"It just ended. We made the quarterfinals."

"Congratulations."

They'd made their way out the door, into the short hallway beside the gym. They nodded and smiled at each other again. "See you around," said Matt. Cameron walked away, down the hall and around a corner. He had an unconscious bounce in his step that Matt had seen before, the proud bearing of the natural athlete. Once again Matt wondered at himself, what had come over him.

A few weeks later, when he received his college board scores, he found he'd done well enough to have some options. In the top tier of his class, bored with high school, eager to follow Mr. Donatello's prodding, he studied the catalogs that came in the mail and read hundreds of course descriptions. He looked for schools that listed courses in social work, sociology, politics, public policy. He talked with his guidance counselor about careers in social work and urban studies, even though he didn't know if he wanted a career, he just wanted to help people. He showed Mr. Donatello a few of the catalogs, but he could tell that the coach was only slightly interested. Seneca was having its best baseball season in years. Big-league scouts were lining up to see their ace pitcher.

Matt's parents cheered his test scores and his excellent grades. They said they'd be proud of him no matter where he went to college. But by late spring he could tell they were growing restless. When catalogs from two nearby Christian colleges arrived, they waited for him to apply to them, and couldn't understand why he continued to explore other schools. Matt's potential majors made them nervous as well. They never talked about it, but he knew. Poverty, the environment, racial equality—his parents genuinely believed those issues were important, but at the same time they associated that sort of thing with the more liberal denominations. Your priorities, after all, said something about what you believed, what you thought the Gospel really meant. Inevitably, the problems you emphasized and the tasks you undertook made you tend toward a certain sort of company. Matt's interests, although his parents couldn't put a finger on anything wrong with them, were foreign to their way of thinking. It would please them most, he knew, if he attended a Christian college and chose a safe, neutral major like chemical engineering.

They arranged a meeting for Matt with Brian Forster, an Ebenezer member who'd graduated several years ago from Steadfast Rock College. While his parents took a walk after the Sunday morning service, Matt and Brian sat down in a back pew. Brian had brought along the latest admissions brochures, all of which Matt had seen. Matt had heard all of Brian's arguments, too, about integrating faith and learning, and forming a Christian worldview. At Steadfast Rock, no matter what your major was, you received a grounding in Bible and common-core Humanities that would benefit you for the rest of your life.

"This is an important decision, Matt," said Brian, resting his hands on his beefy thighs. "You want to make sure you honor the Lord in this matter."

After six years of Will's simple sermons, Matt thought he could use the depth and rigor of some college courses on the Bible. He also liked the idea of using his faith to understand art and culture, and he wanted to know how Christian principles could guide his work on social problems. In some ways, during the years his family had been going to Ebenezer, he felt his mind had stalled. If he was going to make a difference in the world as a Christian, he needed to toughen up his ideas, make them more adult.

But what if going to Steadfast Rock was exactly the wrong way to do that? Wouldn't all the answers be laid out ahead of time, like the points in one of Will's sermons? His parents clearly wanted him to go to Steadfast Rock, the denomination's school, just sixty miles away. He believed in everything the college stood for. But whatever he learned at Steadfast Rock would be filtered through one all-encompassing perspective—threatening the honesty he'd learned among his friends at school, the willingness to admit uncensored experience. He hated the thought of betraying that open, fearless side of himself.

"What's there to do at Belfast Crock?" Mike asked one day, when Matt was in the midst of his deliberations.

"Steadfast Rock."

"Whatever."

"What you do at any college, I guess. Movies, plays, lectures. Concerts."

"Like by Harold Hymnal and his Holy Horde?" suggested Mike. "Or for those with psychedelic tastes, I suppose there's Strawberry Salvation."

"What about you? Have you figured out where you're going?"

Matt thought Mike's decision might be harder than his own. Mike could major in music at any college or university, or he could try to get into a place like Juilliard or Berklee. Or he could skip college altogether, and play his way up from the bottom, gig by gig. He had an uncle who knew a lot of Pittsburgh musicians.

"I got this catalog the other day," said Mike, tossing a thick book over to Matt. "I couldn't believe how many courses they have."

The catalog was from a large state university. Matt flipped to the music department, then looked at political science, sociology, social work. Mike was right. The offerings filled column after column. There were whole courses devoted to topics that a class might cover for a week at Steadfast Rock.

"I see what you mean," said Matt, still turning the pages.

"I thought you might be impressed," said Mike. "A little more there than you'd get at the Rock, huh?"

Hoping to hash the whole thing out once and for all, Matt made a last appointment with his guidance counselor. He prepared a little speech ahead of time, explaining the choice between Steadfast Rock and Channing State. One school offered the clarifying vision of his faith, the other gave a broad, neutral sweep of knowledge. One allowed him to dig deeper into what he believed, the other promised new ideas, unbounded by preconceived notions. When he'd finished describing the two alternatives, he sat back in his chair and waited for guidance.

Miss Crane looked puzzled. She smoothed her skirt and shook back her layered blond hair. After glancing again at the folder in her lap, she smiled up at him and shrugged.

"I'm sorry," she said. "I don't think I understand what you're asking."

Matt hesitated, then tried again. "Basically I've got these two different ways of learning—of studying things—and I'm trying to decide which one I should take."

She nodded. "Well, the way you've described the two approaches to me, it sounds like you've already decided."

"It does?"

"Mm-hmm. Should you go with a pre-packaged set of assumptions and ideas, or should you take on the challenge of thinking for yourself?"

"I don't know if I'd put it quite like that," said Matt.

"No?" She smiled again. "That's the way I heard it. In fact I think you used almost those exact words."

"Well, that might be the case, but for me—" Matt heard his voice getting tense. "To me it's more of a toss-up than that."

Miss Crane frowned down at the folder. She shook her head slightly. "This is where people's backgrounds play a role in their decisions. I can't always be of help when that happens."

"What do you mean?"

"Well, obviously your religious beliefs are very important in deciding what you'll do."

They stared at each other for a moment.

"I guess that's right," said Matt.

"I definitely think that's the way it is. And at that point I really don't have anything to say."

He got out of her office a minute later, his face hot and sweaty, heart pounding. He returned to his study hall and stared at the floor with an open book in front of him. It took a long time to realize that what he felt wasn't shame or embarrassment but anger. He knew what the counselor thought of him—that he was an ignorant, Bible-thumping zealot. As far as she was concerned, he was shackled by a narrow-minded upbringing, sheltered from what his parents and his church considered dangerous ideas. That was how she viewed his most important commitments. That was what people like Miss Crane thought of his faith. After dinner that night he started the paperwork for enrolling at Steadfast Rock.

It seemed to take a long time to get through his senior year. His remaining classes meant nothing to him. Band and Debate Club just cluttered the week. His real life lay ahead at Steadfast Rock, where he would sharpen his tools for making a difference in the world. He visited campus three times, using any excuse to go there and imagine himself a part of the place. By the spring he knew his way around Old Main, the Student Center, the library, his future dorm. He took pride in the dignified old buildings, the elaborate flower beds, the stately trees with roots that heaved the narrow concrete paths. As his graduation from Seneca High approached, he felt even more ecstatic than he'd expected. He laughed when relatives gave him cards and gifts—as though, after he'd just won the lottery, people were chasing after him with more money.

On the night of commencement his class reserved Albert's for a party. The low sprawling building on the outskirts of town had been a hangout for as long as anyone could remember. Dark wooden tables, sticky from decades of spilled pop and barbecue sauce, filled the single open space. When you spotted your waitress bringing your food from the kitchen, it might take her five minutes to reach your table through the chaos. Kids ate dinner with their parents at Albert's sometimes, but pretended not to know anyone, while people at surrounding tables returned the favor. Usually groups of ten or more went for sandwiches after football or basketball games, or on summer nights when they hadn't seen each other for a while.

Matt decided to go to the party—not for one last blowout at the old place, but to keep his good mood going. After the ceremony he changed quickly and headed for Albert's. The cinder lot was already more than half full. He parked his Pinto, bought in part with an early graduation gift from his parents, walked through the night air charged with barbecue and muffled music, and entered the building. They'd moved the tables to create a large space in the middle of the floor, surrounded by buffet tables and places to sit and eat. It looked and sounded a lot like a Seneca High dance.

Picking his way through the dimness, however, he saw that this might actually be fun. Just about everyone he knew had come to the party, except Mike who had a gig with his uncle's band. If he'd wanted to, he could have searched the room and found his usual lunch crowd. Instead he lingered in a noisy gathering near the entrance, in no hurry to get anywhere. Everyone was smiling and laughing. People he'd known since elementary school but hadn't spoken with in years rushed up to him, greeting him by name. All the old cliques and codes had magically disappeared.

Eventually he got a sandwich and a pop at one of the side tables. A girl from Social Problems bumped hips with him in time to the music. Matt held his drink high, trying not to spill. They laughed.

"I'm so happy!" shouted Matt.

"I know!" replied the girl. "Isn't it great?"

They laughed again and separated, moving out into the crowd. Familiar faces surged up from years of half-forgotten experiences—Cub Scouts, a junior high play, day camp the summer after fourth grade, co-workers from various jobs. He felt a wistful, belated affection for all these people.

Turning from a conversation with someone in the jazz ensemble, he stood face to face with pretty brunette Patty LeFleur, who'd been waiting to greet him.

"Well hi," she said.

"Hey!" Matt gave her a one-armed hug, embracing the soft tumble of her hair. Patty had sat in front of him in American Lit, a course neither of them had cared about but that helped fill out their last semester. They'd become friends in the giddy last weeks of slacking off. When the teacher stepped down the hall, leaving the class to write "reflections" on Melville or Poe, Matt and Patty discovered they had identical tastes in music and obscure TV shows. He'd found himself looking forward to the class. Here at the party, amid the flashbacks and the sentimental memories, Patty was current and real, his classmate from just the other day. She looked good, too, in a snug short-sleeved sweater that didn't quite come down to her jeans. He discovered that he'd been expecting to see her.

"Having a good time?" she asked.

"Terrific!"

She raised her eyebrows. "Wow."

"I know," he said. "I didn't expect it. But I'm not looking at a horse . . . what's that expression about looking at a horse?"

"Something about a gift horse's mouth."

"A what?" The music was loud.

"A gift horse!"

"What's that?"

"Never mind."

"Okay. Are *you* having a good time?"

She shrugged. "Sure."

When Patty hadn't gotten into Bucknell, she'd settled for commuting to a Penn State branch, where course offerings and activities would be limited. Their college plans could easily have become a sore point, but Matt had always managed to change the subject. It would be harder on this night of bright futures and goodbyes.

"Come on," he said.

"Yeah, I know." She shook herself and smiled at him. "You'll be two hours away! I'll never see you!"

"It's less than that," he said. "Let's get some more food. Those sandwiches are good."

They loaded their plates and sat at a table away from the dance floor. They laughed about some blunders the commencement speakers had made. Matt retold a couple of childhood stories he'd heard that evening, then for several minutes they listened to the mix of rock, funk, and disco. After the loud and effortful conversations of the last hour, Matt relaxed at Patty's side, wordless and content, watching the shuffling groups on the floor. The music gripped him like a trance, the old collective spell of radio. Lights flashed. Bass notes vibrated through his shoes. Couples merged, revolved, dissolved, resolved. It was perfect. It was chaos. It was all he could want.

When the deejay played "Young Americans," Patty jumped up and said they *had* to dance. They found an open spot on the floor. Dancing, always an awkward social obligation at best, had never come so easily for Matt. He moved without thinking, watching Patty's graceful hips and laughing smile. They stood a few feet apart but danced as one, as effortlessly as clowning around in class.

The song ended. Patty took him by the wrist. "Come here," she said.

She drew him past their table and behind a column, to a shadowy corner strewn with stacked trays and service carts. Putting her arms around him, she kissed him slowly and meaningfully.

"I'm going to college, not a war," Matt laughed.

She kissed him again, moist lips parting. He lowered his face to fit hers. She took his hand and placed it under her sweater. For several seconds they stood like that, mouths locked, his hand under her bra. He forgot everything but the softness, the urgency, the warmth.

"You wanna go somewhere?" she breathed in his ear.

The words seemed to wake him. He withdrew his hand gently, held her hips at bay. He shook his head. Her dim-lit features froze.

"I'm sorry," he said. After a moment he added, "I think I better go."

He stumbled away, toward the door. He just wanted to get out. "*You jerk!*" she shouted after him. He pushed blindly through the throbbing music, the seething crowd. The door flew open, tilted crazily against the stars. The moonlight and the sharp air smote his head. He filled his lungs and ran, soles skidding on cinders. In the Pinto he sat for a gasping, trembling minute. Before he put the car in gear, and the motions of driving dulled his mind, he remembered how Patty's abrupt puzzled stare reminded him of Miss Crane's.

All summer, while he handed clubs and brightly painted balls across the counter at the Stanton Mini Putt, and sat watching kids spin the windmill vanes and crawl through the spouting whale's mouth, he relived those searing minutes with Patty. He never saw her again, of course. He thought about calling her, but didn't know what he could say to make things different. He would still be the same person, no matter what either of them wanted. He'd acted the way that person would have to act. It wasn't a question of whether or not he'd done the right thing.

In the fall, when he'd been at Steadfast Rock for a couple of months, he wondered if he'd ever be kissed again the way Patty LeFleur had kissed him. Within days he felt he knew everyone on campus. Their common faith made everything easy, and he immersed himself in studies, meetings, and meals. Sitting around talking consumed every unscheduled minute. On his dorm floor almost no one closed their doors. To do so was considered rude and antisocial. Guys walked from room to room like it was one big house, flopping on a bed or chair to join one discussion before getting up and wandering off to the next. In the dining hall he sat with his floor mates for the first few weeks, then gradually learned to take his time, carrying his tray among the noisy tables, looking for people he didn't know very well. Someone always welcomed him and offered a place. On some evenings he drank coffee with a friend or two until the dinner shift wound down and the staff came around with buckets and rags.

He hadn't anticipated this part of going to Steadfast. For the first time in his life—aside from one week a year at Bible camp—he lived with people like himself all day long. You didn't need to explain yourself. Everyone believed the same things, shared the same assumptions, obeyed the same rules. Everyone used the same words the same way. If you suddenly felt like singing "Guide Me, O Thou Great Jehovah," then you went ahead and belted it out, whether you were in the shower or walking to class. People prayed before meals, and in their rooms. They had floor Bible studies that overflowed the lounge. Many professors opened the semester with a prayer. All of this, which might once have struck Matt as excessive, felt natural and unconstrained. Christian life together was part of what they'd all come here for. Even when Matt and a few close friends parodied a sanctimonious professor, or rolled their eyes at a classmate's overdone piety, no one questioned the prevailing culture. They were merely laughing at a case of bad form.

In the dorm they talked about girls all the time, more than Matt remembered doing with his friends in high school. They debated whom to ask out, who was way out of reach, who was gorgeous, pretty, cute, sweet. Matt's floor had a long-standing connection with the floor of a neighboring women's dorm. He didn't know how long the relationship had existed, but the two floors threw parties together, traded pranks, and organized midnight study breaks. Matt and his dorm friends, who'd become very close in a matter of months, grew just as close to some of these women. They came to feel like sisters, which naturally discouraged their being asked out on dates. Occasional rumors of drama and recrimination reached his dorm from the second floor of Marshall. Matt himself spurred a tempest of resentment for a few weeks, when he dated a girl from one of the supposedly more glamorous dorms.

On the floor late at night the guys talked about sex in the "Wouldn't It Be Nice" kind of way that virgins talked about sex. At least Matt assumed they were all virgins. No one discussed what actually happened on dates, and most dates took place entirely in public anyway. A movie in the Student Center, a burger in the snack bar, a few daring minutes on a sofa in a crowded lounge—spending time with the opposite sex at Steadfast Rock went more or less along the lines of a Victorian picnic. When Matt heard about a student who became pregnant and left school, he was genuinely mystified as to how such a thing could have happened. In a shadowy corner of memory he cherished Patty LeFleur, his secret shame and pride.

To many of his friends, Matt was a borderline nerd. He studied a lot, and he studied like someone who truly wanted to learn. From his first thoughts about someday going to college, he'd wanted to push himself. He wouldn't be satisfied until he'd thought as hard and learned as much as possible. "The world of ideas" had an almost literal existence for him, a wondrous place of marvelous discoveries. Steadfast Rock, with its library, professors, and cloistered campus, became that wondrous place. His first semester passed in an intellectual swoon. For him, "Further Reading" meant mandatory reading. He showed up at his teachers' office hours, pursuing ideas left hanging during class discussion, requesting yet more reading. If a professor looked quizzical or amused when he asked questions, Matt did not return. He sought the ones who craved knowledge the way he did, unselfconsciously, unafraid of looking driven or strange.

One afternoon he went to the library after his sociology class, and found a little book the professor had put on reserve, a survey of approaches to ending poverty in American cities. It was two hundred pages long. Matt sat down in a carrel by a window, and read the entire book. Although he could tell that the survey would never be a classic, he could also see that it was timely, clear, and succinct. As he read about various proposed strategies, evaluating the arguments for each, he felt himself acquiring a new way of thinking. He began to grasp not only the issues in the book, but the methods his professor used in class. The whole course stood out clearly before him, every lecture a new path, every book a part of the adventure, every assignment fulfilling the design.

Shortly after four-thirty he paused and looked out the window. Bleak November light was fading in the treetops. Lamps blinked on beside the narrow paths. In the dorm the guys would be stirring, collecting a gang for dinner. He would read for another hour. The stacks creaked as students paced above and around him. Lights flickered and buzzed. In the stillness and the odor of books he felt content, in no hurry to end his solitude. When he finished the book, his friends would still be around somewhere. The dining hall would still be serving. He took his time with the final pages, looking up to think, looking out the window to dream, imagining a future of converting ideas into action.

When he got to the dining hall, a few scattered groups sat finishing dessert or in the middle of a late meal. They seemed an older crowd, having trickled in after the first stampede. Matt went through the cafeteria line, and ventured out with his loaded tray. Beside the windows, at an otherwise empty table, sat a junior named Scott Clausen, who motioned toward a chair with his mouth full when Matt asked if he'd mind some company.

Matt couldn't say when or how he'd met Scott. He was one of those people everyone just knew. He was on student government, chapel steering committee, dorm council, yearbook staff. He was easy to talk with, but he had a solemn air about him, perhaps from his majors in Bible and Philosophy, or possibly from his long thick beard. The Clausens had been Steadfast people for generations. Matt thought they came from somewhere in the Midwest.

"Hope I'm not breaking in on any deep thoughts," he said. "Or maybe you're waiting for someone?"

"Nope, nope, nope," said Scott. "Got left behind, that's all." He waited while Matt bowed his head, then asked, "How's everything going?"

It was a sincere question—the concerned upperclassman taking an interest in a student's first year. Matt talked about his classes in a general way, and said he liked life in the dorm.

"Have you joined anything yet?" asked Scott. "We could use you on yearbook."

"Thanks. I don't think I'd be very good at that. Just a feeling, I don't know. I'm trying concert band for now."

Scott looked sympathetic, perhaps guessing Matt's boredom with band. He contemplated Matt through his round wire-rimmed glasses. "You're smart to look around before committing to anything," he said. "You just got here, after all."

This wasn't the way Matt thought of himself, as a wide-eyed new arrival. He decided to strike a more upbeat tone. "I've gotten pretty interested in some of my classes. I like the reading."

Scott nodded, tossing back his shaggy brown hair. Matt told him about being absorbed by the book in the library, his exultant sense of discovery. For the first time, he knew *this* was why he'd come to college. It had been an afternoon he would never forget.

Scott pointed his chocolate-pudding spoon at him and said, "But what about your intellectual growth?"

Matt laughed, taken aback. "I thought that's what I was talking about. Today in the library I was growing intellectually. Trying to, anyway."

"Well, yeah. In a local kind of way. Solving tactical problems, you could call it. But at a higher level, where do you get your perspective on those problems?"

"You mean like how do I know racism is bad, poverty is bad?"

"Think bigger, Dr. Schweitzer," said Scott with a caustic smile. "We need some kind of truth to back up what we do. Otherwise it's just humanistic striving. Without absolute truth, all you've got is irrationalism and the will to power."

Matt had heard this sort of thing in his Bible and Humanities classes. For some reason it irritated him, hearing it over dinner. He didn't see the inevitable link between "humanistic striving" and the will to power. He went after Scott's argument, surprised at how readily the words came. "But don't you think people can find a common ground where knowledge is knowledge, skill is skill, and they can try to get things done whether they're Christians or not?"

"Then why go to Steadfast?" asked Scott.

"The girls from second-floor Marshall?" Matt almost shot back. Instead he said, "Lots of reasons, including the chance to have conversations like this one. Of course I want my work to be grounded in truth, but I think I've still got a lot to learn about where to find that truth."

"Jesus said, 'Sanctify them through thy truth: thy word is truth,'" quoted Scott. After a few minutes he said he had a New Testament exam to study for, and left.

Matt assumed that the absolute truth Scott was talking about was truth from the Bible; but he couldn't write off his years of public school as some kind of humanistic delusion. Mr. Donatello might not have been a Steadfast-approved Christian, or even much of a social theorist, but he'd helped Matt get on a good path. And the book he'd been reading in the library that afternoon—nowhere did the author refer to God or quote the Bible, yet he pointed out clearly the ills of American society, and proposed some likely remedies. As much as Matt believed the Bible, and held dear his memories of Will with his floppy King James, a small insistent voice told him that the Bible didn't have all the answers. A small chill came over him as those words crossed his mind. He would never have put it in quite that way to anyone at Steadfast, and he was almost afraid to put it that way to himself. He was convinced, though, that his faith—as much faith as he possessed—left room for all kinds of knowledge, some of which wasn't in the Bible. In his deepest self he believed that God wanted him to know those things too. Hadn't God created, and didn't God love, that deepest, most honest self?

His first summer of college he worked in the Steadfast library, living in a sublet apartment near campus. His parents approved of his initiative, and liked seeing him strengthen his ties with Steadfast Rock. Matt, too, learned to relish his year-round life at the college. The deep leafy shade and blooming flowers had helped forge his first connection to the place, when he'd visited campus as a prospective student. Now he claimed that summertime campus as his own, while helping Mrs. McCauliffe in the serials department: picking up mail at the Student Center, checking in and distributing new magazines, ordering replacements of lost or damaged back issues. During breaks he sat in the staff room with Mrs. McCauliffe and the others, eating doughnuts and making timid little jokes about the news. He felt like one of the regulars.

Each day he christened the newly arrived magazines, inking and lowering the wooden-handled stamp that said "Steadfast Rock College Library." Some of the publications, like *Christianity Today*, he'd seen at home for as long as he could remember. Others he encountered for the first time—dozens of journals devoted to theology, church topics, Christian life, missions. The covers, titles, even the illustrations and designs, gave him glimpses into how other people believed. He didn't need to study the contents to guess the difference between *Banner of Truth* and *The Christian Century*. Over lunch he sat on a bench outside and read articles that had caught his eye, deciding what he thought about the ecology movement and whether he favored Bultmann or Barth.

He attended the church across the street from campus, where a lot of faculty and students went. On those summer mornings he must have looked lonely and left behind, because members made a point of talking with him after services and inviting him home for Sunday dinner. The young, intellectual pastor reminded him of Scott Clausen, preaching the need for biblical truth against the insidious threat of a rudderless, hedonistic culture. He couldn't get used to the lecture-like sermons, or the pews full of people taking notes. He tried it a few times, but usually ended up doodling.

On two weekends he drove home, where the Ebenezer people greeted him vaguely, unsure where he'd been or even if he'd been away. A few of his parents' closer friends asked how college was going. He learned to keep his answers brief. He'd looked forward to Will's preaching, thinking it would be a refreshing change, but he remembered every word and gesture, each well-worn passage of supporting scripture. Restless and yawning, he avoided his mother's sharp eye.

By the hot dry days of mid-July, the deserted campus had lost its charm, and the library felt like any other job. He missed his dorm friends, and the hectic rush of classes. One afternoon, pushing a cartful of bound periodicals into the basement stacks, he heard someone call his name. He turned around. The voice hadn't sounded familiar. From halfway up the stairs, a face looked down, a face belonging to no one at Steadfast Rock. He stepped closer, peering up through the dimness. It was Ben Cameron, the wrestler from high school.

"Ben!" he exclaimed, as though they were old friends.

Cameron, who'd been climbing the stairs to the first floor, retraced his steps and shook Matt's hand—the ordinary way this time. They stood grinning for a moment, then commented on the odds, running into each other in the nearly empty building.

"What are you doing at Steadfast Rock?" Matt asked.

"I had some reading to do. It isn't that far from State College."

"I forgot, you went to Penn State. You got a scholarship, didn't you?"

"Yeah. I'm spending the summer there, training with some guys."

Matt nodded. He could roughly imagine the jock life Cameron must be living. "But . . . what kind of reading do you need to do here at Steadfast? They do have a library at Penn State, don't they?"

"I think I heard about one once," Cameron mused, deadpan. He smiled again. "It's kind of a long story. See, I turned Christian."

"Wow," said Matt. It sounded stupid, but it was all he could manage to say. No one had told him something like this before. Dramatic conversions only seemed to happen in the Bitter Gulch Boys books he read as a kid. The way Cameron said "turned Christian" kept sounding in his ears. He hadn't heard anyone put it that way. He said cautiously, "You mind if I ask how it happened?"

"I knew some people. I started reading the Bible. After a while I just realized I believed."

Matt wondered if he'd been one of the people Cameron knew. Unlikely, he decided. They'd barely been acquainted. Cameron probably wouldn't have known anything about him. Still, reputations in high school got around. People knew more about you than you thought.

"So how do you like it here?" Cameron asked.

Matt tried to pull his thoughts together. "Oh, I like it a lot. It's been a good place for me, I think."

Cameron nodded. "It seems nice." He still parted his hair in the middle, and kept his eyes narrowed. Matt suddenly recalled standing with the marching band on a practice field, watching Cameron circle the school at a jogging pace, wearing a shiny warmup suit that must have made him sweat a lot. "Making weight," they called it. He still looked lean and wiry, but bigger, more muscular. Their contest on the mat didn't seem remotely possible.

"What kind of stuff do you come here to read?" asked Matt.

"All kinds of Christian things. Theology, sermons, commentaries, spiritual growth. I figured I could find a lot that I was interested in all in one place." He smiled. "I've got some catching up to do."

"Have you found a good place to go to church?"

Cameron winked at him. "Not there yet, bro."

"Ah." Matt had no idea what he meant.

"I should let you get back to work," Cameron said.

"I guess. Hey, let's stay in touch."

They exchanged campus addresses, and Cameron turned back to the stairs. "Guess I'll be seeing you around."

"Great to see you again, Ben."

Through the rest of the afternoon, and later in his stifling apartment, Matt kept thinking about high school, how tough and aloof Ben used to be—the last person anyone would have expected to become a Christian. Matt's friends who'd drunk and done drugs had at least seemed needy. They were the type you heard about, who turned to God when they reached the end of their rope. Ben hadn't been weak. Just the opposite. He went around with his chin and his chest stuck out, an athlete who knew he was good, and didn't care what anyone else thought. He didn't need other people. He certainly didn't need God. Nothing mattered but the next practice, the next match. He'd disciplined his body and mind to meet the challenge. He would take down anyone who got in his way.

Then faith came out of the blue, a miracle. Conversion actually happened. Once a silent, swaggering guy people tried to avoid, Ben was now a believer, "one of us." Matt could not stop thinking about it. He and Ben Cameron spoke the same language now, shared the same hopes, felt the same emotions. All of this in someone he'd met at Seneca High—not at church, a Bible camp, or a Christian college. He shook his head, bewildered and a little ashamed. There was so much he'd been unwilling or afraid to believe.

In the fall he took an introductory philosophy course with Dr. Wei, the only philosophy professor at Steadfast. Matt had expected an overview of the history of philosophy, or a survey of basic issues and how to think about them. He'd prepared to buy a big expensive textbook, with pictures and diagrams, maybe even cartoons. Instead he left the bookstore with paperback editions of Plato, Descartes, Berkeley, Locke, and Hume. Reading the original works astonished him. He spent hours in the library staring at the table, questioning everything he'd thought about tables before. Like a wide-eyed child he wandered through fantastic chambers where the mind tried to prove its existence to itself, or daubed properties onto matter like so much paint, or was duped into believing that matter existed at all. Then Dr. Wei mocked and parodied everything Matt and the class had just read. He used his hero Ludwig Wittgenstein to explode every mad vision that had captivated them the day before.

The performance was entertaining, but Matt couldn't say he followed it in any detail. The class often made him feel like an outsider. The Bible and

Philosophy majors asked long, involved questions, guffawing when Dr. Wei skewered yet another famous philosopher. They looked thoughtful when he refuted arguments with simple analogies that turned out to be, as far as Matt was concerned, ambiguous and hard to understand. They nodded sagely at his modest, understated conclusions. Eventually Matt grew tired of seeing the teacher placed on a pedestal. He wasn't interested in a little club of big ideas, as he thought of it. He knew only that Dr. Wei seemed different from his other teachers at Steadfast, with an intellectual seriousness about him that approached, at last, Matt's shining ideal of college.

One day toward the end of the semester, Dr. Wei set aside the reading list of great philosophers, and discussed a handful of writers whose ideas Matt knew about from working in the library, and from talks with Scott Clausen. These Christian "thinkers," as Dr. Wei called them with faint sarcasm, had influenced people at the college in profound but often unacknowledged ways. Dr. Wei took up each writer, examined his arguments, and flicked him aside the way he'd done with Descartes and Berkeley. He pointed out inconsistencies and contradictions. He exposed fallacies. He scoffed at grandiose claims. He showed how certain lines of thought could lead to absurd, even dangerous conclusions.

Enthralled, Matt scribbled, smiling uncontrollably. "This is great!" he scrawled in the margin, interrupting his notes. "He's really cooking now!" Before his eyes, a faculty member was daring to challenge pervasive college orthodoxy. After weeks of watching his classmates idolize Dr. Wei, Matt finally felt his own deep connection to the man. If it had been possible for him to put his finger on the ways his Steadfast classes left him unsatisfied, he would have come up with something, he felt sure, like what Dr. Wei was saying. It wasn't just a matter of toppling sacred cows and making himself feel superior. Pushing the Steadfast heroes to the side made room for things he really wanted to do, things he wanted to think about. He could tell the truth about the world, without limiting himself to official formulas.

A few days later he checked his mail in the Student Center, and on his way out found Scott Clausen walking beside him. As usual Scott asked how things were going, and Matt mentioned his philosophy class.

"I hear a lot about Dr. Wei," said Scott. "Never took a course from him, though." *And never would*, Matt could hear him silently add.

"He's pretty interesting," said Matt. "I wouldn't call myself a disciple, exactly, but he's got me thinking twice about some things."

"Like what?"

"The whole idea that Christianity is grounded on some rational basis. Is it purely rational to believe in the Bible the way we do? Or at some point does it become a matter of faith?"

"Like leap-of-faith faith, you mean?" asked Scott.

"I don't know," said Matt. "That phrase 'leap of faith' doesn't scare me like it used to. I don't think believing the Bible is based on empirical evidence, but that doesn't mean it's the same as believing in the Easter Bunny."

Scott shook his head. They were standing outside his dorm in a chilly wind, shoulders hunched. Bare branches clacked overhead. "From everything I hear," said Scott, "I'm a bit leery of that guy, that's all I know. I'm just not sure where he's coming from."

Scott seemed willing to leave it at that, but Matt decided to press him. He wanted to have it out with Scott. "Okay," he said. "Let's say there isn't a leap of faith. Say there really is this rational foundation for what we believe. Why is that so great? Who wants a totally rational faith anyway? How is that even faith?"

Scott sighed. He ran his fingers through his beard. His eyes behind his glasses watered with the cold. "You can't just stand out there on thin air," he said. "You have to have an objective basis for what you believe. And that comes from the written Word of God."

"I keep hearing that word 'objective,'" said Matt. "We're supposed to stand up for 'objective truth.' What are we afraid of, exactly? What do we think will happen if we leave a subjective crack or two open here and there?"

Scott said nothing. He looked at Matt as though he no longer recognized him, as though he'd changed into a different person before his eyes. Matt suddenly realized he didn't feel like continuing. He couldn't take that look anymore.

"Hey, I know what you mean," he said, hearing how lame he sounded. "When it comes to everyday life I'm on the same side as you. I don't know anywhere else to go but the Bible. I just get tired of the overconfidence, that's all."

"It isn't overconfidence if you're right," said Scott.

That night Matt had the dream he'd been having all semester. He was wrestling. Nothing more than that—no recognizable opponent, no reason for the contest, no particular place or time. He was just wrestling. In the morning he wouldn't remember the dream. Then the next time he had it he would think, "Of course. Here I am. I'm wrestling again."

II.

THE WORD

"THAT SOUNDS LIKE A nice time," said Ann. "What's your friend's name again?"

"Ben."

"From high school?"

"Originally. We didn't get to know each other until later."

Ann smiled. "Funny how things work out that way sometimes, like people aren't quite ready for each other at first."

She moved around the living room picking up and straightening, running a dust mop over the floors. It was her weekly routine, so having a guest wasn't putting her to any extra trouble.

"You're sure I won't make him uncomfortable?" she asked. "I always assumed it would be a problem for your old friends."

"Not Ben," Matthew said.

When he and Ann had rented the apartment, she reassured him again and again. "I suppose technically we're living in sin," she'd say. "But you know we hardly ever get around to actually sinning." Which in fact was true. When Matthew returned from work Ann would be at the lab. Then he'd be asleep by the time she got home. It felt like they used the bed in shifts. Over time Matthew grew accustomed to an arrangement he wouldn't have dreamed of only a year ago. Now Ann was the one who brought it up, fretting that she'd made him violate his conscience, or that his family and friends would think she was a painted harlot. Matthew just laughed.

They'd met at St. Sebastian's in Center City, several months after he moved to Philadelphia. At first he'd gone to a church that Doug McKeon told him about, which made his parents happy. There he met plenty of people like the people at Steadfast, who took notes during the sermon, joined small-group Bible studies, and knew just about everything about each other. Feeling crowded in an all too familiar way, Matthew tried a larger church with a nationally known pastor and an energetic contingent of young adults. It was a great place to meet women, but otherwise it reminded him of the church across the street from Steadfast. If anything the feeling was more cerebral, the sermons even more like philosophy lectures—and not very closely reasoned philosophy lectures at that, Matthew suspected. Everyone seemed pleased to be going there, proud of the thriving programs and the famous preacher, but Matthew felt unhappy and restless.

He started looking around—really looking around this time, beyond the sort of churches he'd attended all his life. He visited mainline Methodist and Presbyterian churches. He went to large and small nondenominational ones, and a Mennonite church where a woman sent him home with a cherry pie. He attended, once, a Unitarian congregation where he and some of the members drank coffee afterwards and failed to understand each other. More often than the other places, he visited the Episcopalians, Lutherans, and Catholics—not out of some long suppressed craving for liturgy, but simply because he assumed they would differ the most from churches he'd known. He ended up staying at St. Sebastian's.

The service was full of scripture from beginning to end, which immediately eased his concerns. For all the chanting and kneeling and scented smoke, he felt essentially at home, regardless of what the rector preached or the parishioners actually believed. He knew the words and could learn something for the day. It wasn't until he listened to people talk during the fellowship hour that he got his first real surprise. It could have been a cocktail party. They gossiped, talked about movies, made casual sexual references. There was even some socially acceptable swearing. If he mentioned the sermon, or asked what other meetings they had at St. Sebastian's, no one switched to a pious tone of voice. It was just another topic, if a slightly frowned upon and unexpected one. Out of old habit Matthew doubted their sincerity at first, and wondered if they truly cared about spiritual things, but after a few weeks he got used to the natural, unforced talk. It was one of the reasons he decided to stay.

Those first Sundays, standing in a circle of coffee drinkers, he noticed Ann Clyde's sense of humor, and her laugh that carried across the room. When they were introduced, he could tell immediately that she wasn't the least bit interested in making an impression. There she was, her manner implied—take her or leave her. He'd never known anyone less self-conscious. She grew uncomfortable only when other people seemed not entirely at home in their own skin, or showed signs of taking life too seriously. For Matthew her breezy touch was the cure he needed for a lifetime of Gunther Hohenseligs and Scott Clausens.

As he got to know her, Matthew couldn't help thinking that a lot of Ann's confidence came from money and connections. She'd grown up in Massachusetts and gone to private schools before majoring in biochemistry at Swarthmore. By the time he learned these facts about her, he'd been drawn to her spontaneity and her unaffected ways. Her down-to-earth candor was definitely not a pose. But he couldn't forget that she came from an East Coast world of knowing the right people, going to the right parties, saying the right thing. She'd worked hard to put all that behind her, into what she called her "background," but it made a difference, having had it in the first place. She knew things he didn't know, and in Philadelphia, at least, that mattered more than the fact that she knew nothing about being raised in a western Pennsylvania steel town. "Quit pretending you grew up in the sticks," she laughed once, when he told a story about a groundhog wrecking his family's garden. He didn't mention Jim Parsloe's father and his grimy fingernails, or Mike Hargrove asking if he'd heard of a place called Juilliard. If he told her what he knew about living in the sticks she might realize he wasn't pretending, and he didn't think she wanted to know.

Going to St. Sebastian's reminded him how far he was from home, and how much he still had to get used to. The first time he walked into the place, the pictures, statues, and stained glass overwhelmed him. One kind of image or another seemed to occupy every inch of the sanctuary. Each week he discovered a new symbol squeezed into an altar rail, floor tile, or pew. Surrounded by such an abundance of ornamentation, he remembered Doug McKeon saying, when they were planning the Holy Savior building, "We're intended to worship the Lord in the beauty of holiness, not the holiness of beauty." As he'd grown older, Matthew had looked around at the stark walls and windows of Holy Savior, and wondered what was so holy about ugliness. Nevertheless, he was unprepared for the riot of sights and sounds at St. Sebastian's, the "smells and bells" he'd heard people joke about. It took him a long time to stop feeling like a scared visitor.

Instead of taking a cube of bread and a plastic thimbleful of grape juice during communion, he went forward to receive a mysterious wafer in his palm and sip wine from an elaborate chalice. Only after a month of careful observing could he work up the nerve to participate. Even then, he had to cultivate a whole new idea of what was happening. The simple "Do this in memory" of his childhood no longer sufficed. Something more than commemoration took place at St. Sebastian's, he dimly understood, but he wasn't sure whether he grasped all the details, let alone whether he believed in them. He crept to the rail in a daze of uncertainty and guilt.

His quandaries and discomforts weren't confined to Sundays. All week he swung back and forth between giddy freedom and furtive misgivings. He would join some friends for a beer after work, then find himself haunted by his mother's shocked look. He went to political rallies and a demonstration or two, only to feel uneasy around his stridently secular comrades. On several Sunday mornings he skipped St. Sebastian's and slept in, telling himself he must have needed the rest, and by mid-afternoon he was vowing he'd never miss church again.

After his fourth date with Ann, a long afternoon at the Art Museum, she took him to her apartment and matter-of-factly to bed. There was no use trying to disguise his inexperience, but at least he managed to hide his dismay at the fact that she'd obviously done this before. St. Sebastian's wasn't Bible camp, he told himself. Not all Christians did things the same way.

In his own narrow bed at night he tried to grasp what was happening. Perhaps he'd begun to change on that November day in the library, or in Dr. Wei's philosophy class. Or it could have been some sleepy Steadfast Rock afternoon, when the guys from his floor collected everyone to go to the dining hall, and he realized he'd prefer to go an hour or two later, to search out different companions. At some point an independence had stirred, driving him east to Philadelphia to make a difference in the world, to Sundays at tony St. Sebastian's, to Saturdays watching Ann chase dust bunnies across the floor.

He hadn't yet introduced Ann to his parents, and referred to her simply as his girlfriend. When they rented an apartment together he reported his new address as though it were just another place of his own. At some point his parents were bound to figure it out, but he'd deal with that when the time came. If they caught on little by little to the ways he was changing, maybe his living with a woman wouldn't come quite so much as a shock.

At least he could claim continuity in one part of his life. His job at New Prospects was exactly what he'd had in mind when he enrolled in Mr. Donatello's class, and when he read about social problems at Steadfast. He'd found the opening through the college placement program, and got the job because of his excellent grades and his obvious enthusiasm for the work. His boss, Gabe Wurzler, had told him so. Unlike any church or Bible camp or Christian college, New Prospects valued him for his ability and his interests, not for the way he could talk a certain spiritual talk. When he flew to Philadelphia in the spring of his senior year, and talked with Gabe about New Prospects and his own sense of calling, he knew right away that he belonged there, and that they would offer him the job.

Gabe Wurzler was just one of his bosses. Margaret Roberts, the other co-director at New Prospects, assigned Matthew most of his everyday tasks. She laughed as she shook Matthew's hand his first day. "We've got some things in common, Matthew," she said. He just smiled, wondering what he could have in common with a thirtyish Black woman from Philadelphia. Another time she caught his eye and said, "*I* know what you're going through, young man." It turned out that Margaret belonged to a church in the denomination that operated Steadfast Rock. Of the few Black students who attended the college, at least a third came from Philadelphia. Most of them belonged to Margaret's church. Matthew wasn't sure what Margaret meant about what he was "going through," and he hoped she wouldn't grill him about his spiritual life, but he had to admit that he didn't mind stumbling upon a link to his past in the midst of so much that was changing and new. One link wouldn't hurt.

Despite the nervousness her church connections caused him at first, he soon viewed Margaret as a valuable ally and friend. She'd been through at least as much as he had. People at her church were coolly silent about her job, as though she'd taken up with doubtful companions. It was partly "that whole liberal social gospel thing," as she called it, which her friends were quick to perceive in New Prospects. The agency connected employers with minority job seekers, forging ties with local businesses and consulting with prospective employees. People at her church couldn't fault any one aspect of her work, but the whole enterprise had that aura of "humanistic striving" that so bothered people like Scott Clausen and Matthew's mother. On top of that, as Matthew gathered from stray remarks Margaret made, she had to deal with suspicions toward her role as a female executive. She'd heard whispers that being a "career woman" clearly mattered more to her than being the mother of two young children.

To Matthew it was all just empty slander. None of the caricatures fit the Margaret he saw every day, whom he regarded as one of the most capable, common-sense people he'd ever met. She seemed to know everyone in the city, or at least everyone who'd ever given anyone a job, and she made the most of these connections with a grace and diplomacy he endeavored to emulate. More than any abstract professional aptitude, however, what made Margaret truly formidable was a physical mannerism that her colleagues called The Eyebrow. If a personnel director waffled on an oral commitment, or if a client showed signs of throwing in the towel, Margaret's right eyebrow slowly lowered, wickedly curved, until it projected an awesome weight of disapproval and scorn. Few people could withstand The Eyebrow, not even Gabe. Matthew had not yet suffered its torments, and he intended to keep it that way.

As assistant director, Matthew did a little bit of everything—fundraising, communications, PR, outreach, interviews, follow-up, mediation. Gabe and Margaret entrusted him with important projects, but at any moment he might need to drop everything and do some mundane chore. He once drove to a home in West Philadelphia because a client had left for his first day on a job, and forgotten to put out water for his dog. On such errands he became used to finding himself the only white person on the street.

Laura Cantonelli, the fourth member of the New Prospects staff, and the only one technically subordinate to Matthew, came from a large Catholic family in Cherry Hill. She shared an apartment off South Street with two other women. Matthew could never figure out how much of her South Philly accent was real, and how much she put on for the hick from Stanton. On weekends she usually went home to New Jersey, returning with a tin of cookies or half a chocolate cake. Besides answering the phone—with the accent noticeably toned down—Laura handled the paperwork that the business of helping people produced by the truckload. She knew everything. When Laura was there, Matthew rarely needed to ask questions of Margaret or Gabe.

He liked his colleagues, and saw them outside the office now and then. He made friends at St. Sebastian's, who introduced him to other people recently out of college, and he got to know several of Ann's grad school friends. After a year he was almost always busy on weekends, going to movies, concerts, parties. He lost touch with most of his friends from high school and Steadfast Rock. Mike and his guitar had vanished in California. Scott Clausen worked for an institute that produced Christian books and tapes and kept Matthew on their mailing list, sending him a steady stream of catalogs and appeals. He buried them in the trash before Ann could see them.

His friend Ben Cameron fit no category, no period of Matthew's life. Although they'd met, in a way, at Seneca High, and found each other again at Steadfast Rock, neither school supplied anything like a common background. After Ben materialized that afternoon on the library staircase, he and Matthew became friends through a mutual obsession rather than any social context. They exchanged letters fairly regularly, and got together a few times. Their topic, inevitably, was God.

"I know I must really believe and not be kidding myself," Ben wrote, in the first letter Matthew received from him, "because I would find it a hell of a lot easier *not* to believe. Something real must be making me go to all this trouble." Matthew had always assumed that converts were granted a honeymoon of sorts, an interval of forgiveness, contentment, and peace. Life became a confident walk with God, freed from all the old worries and fears. From what he could tell, it hadn't happened that way with Ben. He'd changed—no question about that—but instead of resting in the certainty of his new faith it seemed he'd undertaken a strenuous labor: seeking the face of God. Bible verses and tried-and-true Christian formulas wouldn't satisfy him.

Some four years after his conversion, Ben still hadn't joined a church. He wasn't comfortable with the way Christians talked, he said. The buzz words and the expected phrases embarrassed him. From the first time he heard them they rang false in his ears. "The Lord put it on my heart." "Lift them up in prayer." "Invite Jesus to be your personal savior." He refused to talk that way, he said, and he figured that must mean he couldn't belong to a church, because churches were groups of people who recognized each other by the words they used. Matthew wanted to object that at St. Sebastian's that wasn't the case—if anything, they didn't have *enough* ways of talking about God—but he didn't want Ben to think he was recruiting him. Besides, Matthew hadn't been going to St. Sebastian's long enough to be sure that there wasn't some subtle, pervasive code. It took a while to recognize the language of a place.

With no set way of speaking to define their path, and no group to keep them in line, Matthew and Ben made up their own way. They took their inspiration from the likes of Kierkegaard, Tillich, Barth, and the Niebuhrs, all of whom Ben started reading in college and still found time to read, despite the demands of his assistant coaching job. He quoted Bonhoeffer,

Gutierrez, Merton, and assorted mystics, and lent Matthew his favorite, heavily marked books. Matthew felt like he was encountering Christianity for the first time. "What *is* faith?" Ben would ask. "A correct thought? An emotion? An obedient act? What's the *difference* between works and faith— putting aside the question of which one God prefers? What does following Jesus really mean?"

"I don't know," Matthew said, a little dizzy but elated. They talked to a standstill, then talked some more.

On the weekend of Ben's visit the Phillies played a series with the Pirates. Matthew had bought tickets for Saturday night and Sunday afternoon. On a clear, cool evening in early June, after Ben dropped his old gym bag off at the apartment, they took the Broad Street subway to Veterans Stadium and settled into their seats on the first-base line. Ben sipped his beer and looked around.

"It's exactly like Three Rivers," he said after a few moments.

He was right, Matthew suddenly realized. Riding the subway from Center City on his trips to Phillies games, he'd thought only of how different the settings of the ballparks were. The Vet rose from a sprawling system of parking lots on a plain just south of the city, while Three Rivers Stadium crowned the tip of Pittsburgh's Golden Triangle, a convergence of rivers, fountains, and bridges. Inside, though, the differences really did disappear. The same concrete tiers of plastic seats ringed the same patchwork of red dirt and artificial turf. It took someone like Ben, only a casual baseball fan, to notice.

For Matthew the details inside the ballpark didn't matter, he just loved the pre-game rituals. He sat back to watch while Ben studied the scoreboard and checked out the neighboring fans. In the outfield, tiny men played catch across enormous distances, throwing the ball in powerful flat arcs. The pitcher's warmup tosses pounded the catcher's mitt while the umpire looked on. Two players sprinted down the sideline, slowed, turned around, and strolled back to their starting place, chatting all the while. Behind home plate, a stadium employee adjusted the microphone for a teenage girl who waited to sing the national anthem.

Matthew and Ben had agreed to root for the Pirates, for old times' sake, but Matthew felt his true allegiance rising to the surface. Over the past year he'd developed a local's fervent loyalty to the Phillies. He could rattle off the stats of his favorite players and describe their quirks on the field. In the top of the first he pointed to where the right fielder stood in an unusually shallow location.

"See how close in that guy is playing?" he said. "Sometimes on a hard grounder he'll try to throw the runner out at first. He's done it a couple of times."

"He can do that?" said Ben.

"Sure. He's got a really strong arm."

"No, I mean is it legal?"

"Of course it's legal," Matthew replied.

He'd answered more brusquely than he intended. It hit him that he'd just used a condescending tone while talking sports with a renowned wrestling champ, now an assistant coach of a college team.

"It *is* a pretty unusual play, though," he added.

Ben laughed. "Just go ahead and say I'm dumb!" he said. "You know I don't know jack about this game!"

In the third inning, with Phillies on second and third and nobody out, Mike Schmidt came to the plate. He twitched his bat and surveyed the field while the organist belted out "Charge." The crowd roared. Matthew leaned forward in his seat.

"What do you think about the Word?" asked Ben.

Matthew sat back, his eyes still on Schmidt. He'd been prepared for something like this. He just didn't think it would happen during a third-inning rally.

"What about it?" he said.

"What does it mean? What *is* the Word of God?"

Matthew tried to think. "Are you asking if the Bible is the Word of God?"

"I'm asking 'What is the Word of God?' If you say 'The Bible,' then yes, I'm asking if that's the right answer."

"I'm not sure if I *do* say 'The Bible,'" said Matthew.

"All right then," said Ben, sounding a little surprised.

In letters, and once or twice when they had talked during college, they'd begun discussing this topic. Someday, Matthew had always known, they would try to get to the bottom of it. Ben had read a lot of Karl Barth, and knew the arguments in detail. Without the same firsthand knowledge, Matthew grasped the basic battle lines, and understood what was at stake. He felt the issue in his bones from a lifetime of doctrinal squabbling, from hearing the anger, pain, and fear in people's voices. *Was* the Bible the Word of God? Or did it—when read or proclaimed in certain ways—"contain" the Word of God, "become" the Word of God? At Steadfast, those despised terms were thought to drive a wedge between the Bible and truth, inserting a layer of subjectivity and whim. Who could say what the Word of God might turn out to be, if it wasn't the plain words on the page—if it emerged as the result of some mysterious "becoming"? Gone was the objective basis for belief. Gone were the rational underpinnings of the faith. Matthew could see Scott Clausen shaking his head.

But it had been years since he'd cared what Scott Clausen thought. "The Word of God" was an open question now. Old bogies like "subjectivity" and "whim" no longer frightened him. He was ready to sort the matter out in bold new terms, and over the last few years that had come to mean sorting it out with Ben.

"Remember who John—or whoever—said the Word is," said Ben. "Jesus Christ is the Word. Jesus Christ is the Word of God."

Matthew watched a guy two rows ahead of them glance back. It happened a lot during conversations with Ben.

"I remember," said Matthew. "But couldn't the Bible *also* be the Word of God?"

"That's always seemed a little fishy to me," argued Ben. "Kind of like saying that this old royal building in London is Buckingham Palace, but this log cabin in Vermont is Buckingham Palace too. Why say that Jesus Christ is the Word of God, and then call a hodgepodge book of writings the same thing?"

Matthew said, "I'm not sure how I feel about comparing the Bible to a log cabin in Vermont."

"Yeah," agreed Ben. "I'm not sure how I feel about that either."

For a minute Matthew stared, unseeing, at the field. "How about this," he said finally. "There's Buckingham Palace, right? And then there's this other old house somewhere, full of memories, beautiful furniture, and fine works of art. It's been in the same family for centuries. The people who live there feel at home. They go from room to room as it suits their mood, finding everything they need whenever they want it. It's an old familiar friend that keeps them company throughout their lives, and never lets them down." He paused. "But it's no Buckingham Palace."

Ben laughed again, and saluted Matthew with his beer. "Not bad," he said. "Where did *that* come from?"

"I don't know. Maybe it's just how I feel about the Bible, after living with it my whole life."

Ben nodded. "Then I guess I've got something to look forward to," he said.

When Matthew paid attention to the field again, the Pirates were at bat and there was still no score. Somehow Schmidt and the Phillies had managed to strand the two base runners.

Over breakfast the next day, Matthew read about the Phillies' loss while Ann and Ben did the crossword puzzle. As he'd predicted, Ben wasn't at all uncomfortable with Ann. After they'd finished the puzzle they talked shop about their universities—Ann was working on her Ph.D. at Penn, and Ben was coaching at Laurel University, an hour or so away. They compared notes on how much funding their respective programs received, with none of the tension that might have come up if Ben had coached football or basketball instead of wrestling. Ann saw Ben as a fellow budget casualty, making do with slivers of the fiscal pie. At around ten, she looked at her watch and stood up. "You guys coming to St. Sebastian's?"

Matthew and Ben looked at each other. Matthew detected a tiny shake of the head.

"I don't think so," he said. "We'll just walk around a little, then head back to the Vet."

Ann shrugged. "Sounds good." She gave Ben her most charming smile. "If I don't see you again, it was great to finally meet you. The sofa was okay?"

"It was fine," said Ben, rising to shake her hand. "Thanks for everything."

She looked at Matthew and gestured toward the breakfast things. "Can you—?"

"Sure," said Matthew.

She leaned to kiss him, and left a few minutes later.

Matthew and Ben took their time finishing breakfast and reading the last sections of the paper. Then they stepped outside into another sunny, comfortable day. They walked to Society Hill and strolled past the old houses with their dainty little trees in front and their porches enclosed by iron railings. Showy flowers spilled from planters. Sleepy cats stared from windows and window boxes. It still felt strange to Matthew, finding so many people out on a Sunday morning, everyone dressed in shorts and T-shirts.

"When you do go to church," he asked Ben, "where do you go?"

"I try to pick ones that won't feel too awful," said Ben. "A few have been okay, but not so I wanted to go all the time." He sidestepped a pretty woman in a sundress and returned her smile. "The only place I go to even close to regularly is the college chapel."

"Lowest common denominator?"

"That's about the size of it."

"I've been meaning to ask you something about the Word of God," said Matthew. "What do you think about that passage in Hebrews?"

"Back up," said Ben. "What passage? I haven't been at this as long as you have, you know."

That was Ben being modest. Or did he just not like to admit how thoroughly he'd immersed himself in the scriptures? In only a few years he'd mastered the Bible, referring to it constantly in letters and conversation. He had pages and pages at his fingertips, almost like Will at Ebenezer.

"*You* know," said Matthew. "'The word of God is quick, and powerful, and sharper than any two-edged sword.'" The King James phrases came out automatically. "I heard that verse a million times growing up."

"Oh, right. That one. And people told you that was about the Bible?"

"Uh huh. All the time. I remember the passage coming up whenever someone wanted to talk about how important the Bible is, how you can't escape its authority and truth."

"Well that's just . . . stupid," said Ben. "Sorry, I don't know how else to say it."

"Why is it stupid?"

Ben sighed a little. "I know you've read the whole chapter, so you know it's full of warnings against disobedience and unbelief. In that context 'the word of God' means God's judgment, the way he can see through excuses and separate truth from lies."

"Yeah, okay," said Matthew. "But then why say 'the word of God,' and not the eyes of God or simply the judgment of God? *Couldn't* the Bible be the word of God that pierces and divides—in the sense of convicting, like people say now?"

Ben shook his head. "I don't think so. I think in Hebrews the word of God is the same as John's Word of God—Jesus Christ, the Word that spoke Creation. *That* kind of powerful. That kind of overwhelming and irresistible."

For a few moments Matthew took this in, adjusting to a different way of looking at the verse. "I guess I see what you're talking about," he said. All of a sudden, though, he remembered another verse. "But then," he hurried on, "Paul says we need to be armed with 'the sword of the Spirit, which is the word of God.' Couldn't *that* sword be the Bible?"

"All right, all right!" Ben said, laughing. "If you really want to, go ahead and call the Bible a sword, and say it's the Word of God!"

"I'm not sure I do want to say that. At least, not the way I always used to hear people say it."

"That's one advantage I have definitely got over you," Ben said. "I don't have to deal with a bunch of old voices in my head."

"They do get pretty loud sometimes," said Matthew.

They'd made their way east from Society Hill to Penn's Landing, where beneath an enormous pavilion people were gathering in front of a stage. Matthew and Ben drew closer to see what was happening. From the crowd a voice called Matthew's name. He spotted Margaret Roberts waving, standing with her husband and two small children. Matthew and Ben walked over to join them.

"Hey," said Matthew. "What's going on?"

Margaret mentioned a band whose name he didn't recognize. "I guess they're a famous jazz group," she said. She nodded toward her husband. "*He* wanted to see them."

"Desmond Roberts," said her husband, shaking hands with Matthew and Ben.

"We rushed away from church," said Margaret, "so they better be good."

Her navy-blue suit looked dressier than her usual work clothes. So did the shiny gold hoops in her ears and her red high heels. Desmond and the kids were dressed up as well. Tyson, who looked about six, had removed his clip-on tie and was whipping it in a circle around his finger. His little sister Winnie sucked her thumb and stared at Ben.

"Ben and I are killing a little time before heading to the ballgame," said Matthew.

"You should stick around a while and hear these guys," Desmond said. "They really are something else."

"Desmond plays," explained Margaret.

"Tenor sax," said Desmond.

"I *love* jazz," said Ben. "I hardly ever get to hear any live."

Matthew sadly recalled marching with his baritone horn in a hundred parades and half-time shows, playing "Brandy" and "Feelin' Stronger Every

Day." So much time, so much pointless movement. So little making of actual music.

They settled into a row of chairs, with Ben and Desmond side by side discussing records and musicians. Matthew told Margaret about Ben. "Well praise the Lord!" she said, when he got to their reunion in the library.

"It's been nice to have a friend like him," said Matthew. "He makes me think about things."

Margaret nodded sagely. "The Lord puts those people in our lives. *And he gives us to* them."

"I guess."

"You guess?" she exclaimed in mock dismay. "What do they teach you at that college anyway? Maybe I need to reconsider my annual check."

"Maybe," said Matthew. "Look at me, a Steadfast alum, skipping church and profaning the Lord's day."

Margaret gave his shoulder a little push. "I was just teasing."

A quintet walked onto the stage, led by a Black saxophonist in sunglasses and a checked fedora. The crowd cheered. Desmond smiled and nodded. The frontman made a little speech and the music started. Matthew watched Ben and Desmond listen with the same intent expression. He enjoyed the tight blend of horns on the opening melody, but his mind wandered when the improvised solos began. Beside him, Margaret gazed around at the crowd, faintly smiling. On Matthew's other side, Tyson jumped and fidgeted. Matthew smiled at him and nodded a few times.

He checked his watch. They would miss at least the first two innings, but that didn't matter, just so everyone had a good time. Ben's visit had gone well so far, he thought. He still didn't know quite what to make of his friend. What was it like being a Christian without belonging to a church? Could reading a lot of books, by itself, help you decide what to believe? He didn't know if Ben prayed very often, or read the Bible in a regular, devotional way, or had any other friends who were Christians. Matthew liked to think he'd left rules and expectations behind, but he couldn't fathom believing with no structure at all. Ben's way seemed as loose and made up as the music.

He smiled. He was reminding himself of his mother. Tyson smiled back at him, and pounded on his knee. Margaret caught the boy's fist and gave him The Eyebrow. What would Scott Clausen say about Ben? What would the Steadfast professors in Humanities and Bible say—the ones whom Dr. Wei liked to challenge and mock? To their way of thinking, Ben just floated along aimlessly, one stopping place as good as another. He had no scriptural authority for his conclusions, no doctrinal framework to guide his life. Everything was makeshift, piecemeal, a collection of hunches and moods. So why did Matthew find Ben's way so compelling? He kept wanting to ask him things, find out how he lived, learn what sort of terms he was on with God. Maybe what floating really meant was not being tied down, not clinging to a system. Maybe Ben had learned to experience something that went beyond the pages of a book. What actually mattered, after all: the word or the Word, the Bible or Jesus?

Beyond the cool shade of the pavilion, trees and buildings shimmered in the heat. Glass and chrome flickered and glared. Inside, the canopy diffused a gray light over the crowd, mingled with the spiky phrases and dense chords of the music. The piano and trumpet intertwined in an agitated flurry, while the sax repeated an infectious riff. Matthew didn't know if he would ever understand jazz, but he thought he might be learning how to listen to it. He glanced down the row of seats at Desmond and Ben. Winnie slept soundly on Ben's lap, head resting on his chest. Desmond caught Matthew's eye, shrugged, and smiled.

Matthew thought back to the way Winnie had stared at Ben when they first arrived. She'd seemed fascinated, as though in that moment she'd chosen him as her favorite adult. A few years ago, Matthew had watched a Steadfast Homecoming parade with some alumni who had brought their young children. With no encouragement from Matthew, a four-year-old boy broke into a huge grin when he saw him. He grabbed Matthew's hand, chattering about his toys and his dog. He wound up on Matthew's shoulders, watching the floats and convertibles go by. It had been fun, but Matthew had always puzzled over the connection. Had he done something? Was it something about the way he looked? Now Winnie and Ben seemed to be sharing a similar instant bond. For several moments Matthew contemplated the pair, the trustful little girl with her thumb in her mouth, the wrestling coach absorbed in the music. He wondered if Ben had some mysterious quality that drew kids to him. Perhaps it was even a spiritual affinity, the child-like faith that Jesus demanded. Little children saw themselves in Ben. Like them, he had a simple, direct connection to God. Abruptly, Matthew set aside the strange thought.

That evening, after Matthew had seen Ben off at 30th Street Station, he and Ann ate at the pizza place around the corner from their apartment. Matthew hadn't taken the sheets off the sofa bed yet, or washed the dishes.

He and Ann agreed to go out and escape the mess. He could tell she wasn't particularly happy about it, but at least it was their favorite pizza. With only two other tables occupied, a Sunday-evening stillness filled the room. They'd come here on one of their first dates, and the place still gave them a nostalgic, romantic feeling. They forgot about work and household chores. Matthew thanked Ann for helping out with hosting Ben.

"You're welcome," she said. "He seems like a terrific guy. What did you talk about all weekend, anyway?"

"We talked some about work. I learned what wrestlers do during the summer."

"Did you talk about me?"

"Of course."

Ann laughed. "I came in right behind Martin Luther and the Apostle Paul, right?"

"We did talk some theology," Matthew admitted.

"I thought that was the whole point about Ben. You told me he's this intense guy who talks about religion all the time."

"I wouldn't say Ben is intense, exactly. 'Intense' is what I've been trying to get away from these last few years. And I probably bring up religion as much as he does. It's something we have in common."

"You and I have religion in common," she said, in a more thoughtful voice, "but it isn't the same."

"No, it isn't the same."

"Why is that, I wonder?" Ann looked at him, fidgeting with the plastic marker that bore their order number. "I think a lot about the day I met you at St. Sebastian's. I remember telling myself, 'This guy's super serious about religion.'"

Matthew shrugged. "Isn't it worth being serious about?"

"It's different with you. Like you and your friend talking about theology all weekend. It's like there's always a lot of drama."

After a moment Matthew asked, "What do you mean by 'drama'?"

"You know. Blowing something up so it's bigger than ordinary life. Making it into this major deal that takes priority over everything else."

Matthew looked at her, and thought she might be a little afraid of him. They weren't fighting, although the nostalgic mood had definitely evaporated. They weren't even arguing. He couldn't win her over by making the right logical points. All he could do was explain the way he saw things, and hope she understood. "I don't want religion to be abnormal or get overblown," he said. "Like when I used to hear people say 'Give your life totally to Christ,' or 'Go bananas for Jesus.' That sort of thing." He shuddered. "But at the same time I think that faith in God *is* abnormal. I mean, it's definitely out of the ordinary, compared to doing your laundry or going to the store. You're talking about . . . God."

Ann studied the number in her hands. She was silent for a long time, head bent, straight blond hair hiding her face. "Sometimes," she said at last, still without looking at him, "I wonder if you've changed very much from the way you grew up."

He thought of his mother: "Sometimes I wonder if you're a Christian at all." He'd thought back then that nothing could make him feel worse. Now he wasn't sure.

Ann kept looking down as their pizza arrived and the woman rearranged things on the table. Matthew waited until they were alone, started to say something, then found he had no idea what he wanted to say. After another minute or two he asked her about the experiment she'd been working on. They talked about their work, their plans for the week. They said nothing more about Ben's visit.

For the next few days he did more than his share of chores around the apartment. He straightened up a pile of books and mail he'd neglected, cleaned the bathroom, scrubbed the kitchen floor. He even cooked Ann's favorite lamb curry one evening when he knew she'd be home. They relaxed, went to a movie, made love for the first time in many days.

During his first summer in Philadelphia, he'd spent a lot of energy adjusting to city life and a new job. The pace of life after college had caught him off guard, and the heat and humidity felt worse than in the western part of the state. He'd had his hands full getting his bearings and managing to survive. This summer he was able to enjoy himself. The weather didn't bother him anymore, and he took advantage of festivals and other events that helped city people get through the summer. He knew the places where people went to get away. He asked Ann if she wanted to go to the Shore or the Poconos for a few days, but she just groaned and shook her head. At the lab there was no such thing as time off. So he thought about taking some vacation time for himself in September. He could go and see Ben, who'd offered to show him around the town and university.

He and Ben exchanged several letters over the summer. Ben was making himself take a break from wrestling, spending most of his time reading, puttering in his yard, and hiking. He'd been seeing a woman he'd met at a party in town, but it didn't sound serious. Eventually his letters always shifted into what Matthew thought of as "epistle mode," taking up a question that one of them had been thinking about, or pursuing some problem they'd stumbled on together. They'd exchanged similar letters shortly after running into each other at Steadfast, but now Ben wrote in more detail, drawing on deeper reading. He also drew from a deeper well of spiritual experience. It had been four years, after all. Like Matthew, he'd had some time to sort through what he believed.

Sometimes Matthew thought he had a rough idea of how the Israelites must have felt when Moses came down from Mount Sinai. During this summer away from coaching and from people in general, Ben seemed as though he spent most of his time with God. Then he would report back to Matthew, in letters that, far from sounding awestruck, described these encounters in a muted, matter-of-fact way. Matthew hung on every word, strangely compelled. When he asked Ben where these revelations came from, the replies were patient but brief. "You do believe in the Holy Spirit, right?" Ben wrote once. To Ben, the insights he arrived at were nothing special. They came to anyone who would listen.

You asked about prayer, Ben wrote in late July, after he'd been camping in the Lehigh Valley. *You have to remember, I started from scratch. I didn't have years of Sunday school and church, like you did. The only prayers I heard were at the dinner table when I stayed at a friend's house, or before a meet now and then, or at graduation. I had no idea how an ordinary person would pray on an ordinary occasion. It really bothered me. How in the world do I talk to God, assuming I can get up the nerve? After visiting a few churches I learned that some people used liturgical prayers, and others used the 'spontaneous' 'Jesus we just want to lift up your name' kind of prayers, which of course are just another kind of liturgy. I figured that for personal prayer most people probably used a variation on one of these types, and I wanted no part of either one. So that was basically my dilemma, starting out. I knew I wanted to pray, but I didn't know a good way to do it.*

You'll be surprised when I tell you how I finally broke the ice. I used the Bible. Not as my reason to pray, or my command to pray, or some guarantee that my prayers would be answered—I used it for the prayers themselves. Come to think of it, that won't surprise you, because you know the Psalms. 'Hear my prayer, O Lord; let my cry come to thee!' 'O Lord, our Lord, how majestic is thy name in all the earth!' 'Remember not the sins of my youth.' 'Establish the work of my hands.' These were my first prayers. I could say the words and mean them, without feeling embarrassed. After a while I dared to paraphrase a little, personalizing them I guess you could say, fitting the words closer to what I felt and meant. I started to be my own psalmist. From there I went to other places in the Bible, like when Paul (or whoever) prays for his friends or for the person he's writing to. I prayed the prayers of Paul, substituting the names of people I know. I've prayed for you that way.

Matthew read slowly. He stopped and reread. He stifled an impulse to underline or scribble in the margins. At first he kept the letters in a big unmarked envelope, tucked among old receipts and bills where Ann would never look. Then, when he found himself referring to them often, he kept the letters near his Bible. But that didn't seem right either. He ended up putting them on a shelf beside some poetry books and favorite novels.

It still made him pause when Ben said things like "Paul (or whoever)" or "the Johannine tradition." Ben had read a lot of higher criticism of the Bible, learning the latest theories about the authorship and historical accuracy of the scriptures. He didn't take every Bible story at face value, the way Matthew always had and still tended to do, at least at first glance. From time to time Ben would interrupt himself and say with a smile, "Of course, it probably didn't happen quite that way." It still gave Matthew a small shiver to admit those kinds of doubts about the Bible. He couldn't help it. He supposed that, thanks to his upbringing, he would always have that troubled voice in his head. He consoled himself that he wasn't the first person to have to deal with his inner fundamentalist.

No matter how far Ben went, though, and he went pretty far, he never wavered about the things Matthew considered essential. God was God. Jesus was the Christ, the Son of God, the Redeemer and Lord. The Holy Spirit was real, prayer was real, the Church, the forgiveness of sins, the coming of the Kingdom—all real. If anything, Ben believed more strongly than Matthew. Where Matthew's lifelong familiarity with these doctrines could make them feel automatic or even worn out, for Ben they were immediate and new. He'd found in them something direct and powerful, while Matthew groped toward a life beyond the words, still dragged back by the old systematizing ways. As a new convert, Ben had vaulted over all the verbiage. Despite Ben's protests that he was just a newcomer bringing up the rear, it was Matthew who felt like he was slipping back, always trying to catch up with Ben.

No wonder Ann couldn't understand. If she got Ben at all, she saw him as a crazy John the Baptist in a wrestler's singlet, or as an amateur (and therefore fake) theologian with an irritating pious streak. In short, he jostled her spiritual equilibrium. With her sneaking suspicion that Ben was just another zealot, Ann struck Matthew once again as the flip side of his mother—who the one time he tried to discuss Ben with her exclaimed, "Oh, honey, he sounds awfully liberal, don't you think?"

It was Margaret who helped him decide what he thought about Ben. He saw her less often during the summer, when she and Desmond took turns looking after Tyson and Winnie. When Gabe traveled to conferences, or went on vacation, Matthew was often left in charge with Laura Cantonelli, and they played loud music and goofed around. The phone rang less often. Fewer clients dropped in. On sleepy afternoons Matthew overhauled the file cabinets, or updated lists of prospective employers. Once he even re-potted the plants.

Early one morning Margaret stopped beside Matthew's desk and fixed him with a meditative stare. "Have lunch with me today, Matthew," she said. "I want to talk with you." For about five seconds he thought he must have done something wrong. Then he realized that her bossy tone was just her way of making him comfortable about having lunch with an attractive married woman.

She'd decided ahead of time where they would go, steering him toward a sandwich place a few blocks away that he'd always meant to try. They stood in line to order and pay—separately—then found a table where they had to wait another ten minutes for their food. "It's worth it," Margaret apologized.

"I'm looking forward to it," said Matthew.

After the server had brought their orders, Matthew wondered whether Margaret was the type who said grace in public. Doug McKeon used to boom out a long formal prayer in the middle of a packed Stanton restaurant. But Margaret paused only a moment, eyes open, before starting her grilled chicken salad. Silently Matthew offered his own thanks.

His corned beef sandwich exceeded his hopes. They ate happily, singing the praises of the meal. With his usual ravenous midday appetite, he savored his food and took in his surroundings. A few dozen tiny tables crowded the place, with spindly chairs on which men in suits and women in chic dresses talked and laughed over mounds of sandwich wrappers. He felt swept up in the hustle and chatter of a vast enterprise. He loved his job. He loved the big city.

"Have you and Laura been behaving yourselves?" Margaret asked.

"Not at all," Matthew replied. "At least that's what the cops keep saying."

Margaret laughed, fingering the gold cross at her throat. "Actually, Matthew," she said, "I take it for granted that you're being *good*. You and I know that's not the most important thing."

He waited, telling himself he was ready for anything.

"Ever since I found out we had Steadfast Rock in common," she said, "I've meant to have a talk about—well, spiritual things, I guess you could say. Maybe it's just as well that it's taken me so long. You can tell me what your life's been like for the past year."

Since his graduation from Steadfast, no one had talked with him this way, about *his life* and *spiritual things*. Part of him was ready to panic and run out the door. Another part, relaxed and at home, knew exactly what she was talking about. He put his sandwich down, deciding how to answer. Margaret's gaze expressed real concern. He had no doubt that she wanted what was best for him. But what did she think was best for him? Lots of people had opinions about that—opinions that made his heart pound and his limbs go cold. He saw something else, something softer than concern, in Margaret's face. She didn't want to tell him what to do. She hadn't asked him here to get him in line. It was only later, thinking it all over at his desk, that he realized what that softness was. It was tenderness. He thought it must come from her being a mother.

"I've been going to St. Sebastian's," he said.

Margaret's face was unreadable. He'd been braced for a stern frown, maybe even The Eyebrow.

"It's an okay place," he went on. "I've met some nice people there." He would not talk with Margaret about Ann. "I'm not sure if I'll . . ."

He made a vague gesture and picked up his sandwich. Margaret might have nodded. For a minute they ate in silence.

"Your friend Ben," she prompted. "I enjoyed meeting him at Penn's Landing."

"Yeah, Ben," said Matthew. "I guess the truth is I'm looking for something more. Ben helps with that."

"I knew somehow—when you told me about him—he was someone the Lord wanted you to know."

Matthew nodded. "It struck me when you said that. I knew you were right."

"Well? What's come of it?"

He hesitated. "Tell me something, Margaret. There's this thing Ben and I talk about. What do you think when someone says 'the Word of God'?"

"I think of the Holy Bible."

"Anything else?"

"What do you mean?"

"Well, Ben says Jesus Christ is the Word of God. Like at the beginning of the Gospel of John."

"Oh," said Margaret slowly. "Yes. That's right."

"He says that's the main meaning—the one we should think of first. Jesus is the Word that God speaks to human beings, the Word he spoke when he made the world."

"Mm-*hmmm*," Margaret said. "Yes. I like that."

"Me too. But then—where does that leave the Bible?"

"I think the Bible is the Word of God too."

"Yeah, that might be what I think. I'm not sure."

Margaret laughed softly, spearing a piece of chicken. "Ooh, you don't talk that way at *my* church. At my church the Bible is the *Word*."

Matthew laughed with her. "That's how it's been at most of the places where I've gone, too. Until St. Sebastian's anyway."

This was going pretty well, he thought. He'd wondered whether at some point he might get nervous, even start to sweat. He'd thought Margaret might try to catch him in some kind of heresy, maybe even guess about Ann. He was pretty sure his living with Ann wouldn't go over very well with Margaret. But he wasn't worried that Margaret might "confront" him, as some people put it. Instead he wanted only to keep on talking, both to listen to his own thoughts and to find out hers.

"There's a way they talk about the Bible at Steadfast Rock," he began.

"Yes?"

"It's like the Bible is the final proof of everything. Absolute truth. The only truth. The Bible, every inspired word of it, is the only way to know anything, so it's like the foundation for everything else."

Margaret had been nodding as he spoke. "Some people at my church talk that way."

"What do you think?"

She shrugged. "I don't know. I don't think I *need* to know. For me it's enough to say the Bible is the Word of God. It's true. All the rest . . ." She stopped with a sly smile.

"All the rest?"

"That's for those *men* to worry about!"

Matthew burst out laughing. "Exactly! I've been dealing with those men all my life." He hesitated again, then said, "I didn't realize they were at other places too."

"Like in a Black church, you mean? Oh yeah, we've got them. My church can be emotional, sure. You wouldn't be comfortable with the style. But whether it's the Steadfast influence or whatever, there's also a heavy theological side. It's the same thing you're talking about. I'm sure it is."

"Huh," said Matthew, interested. "But you don't buy it?"

"I don't know if I buy it or not. It's just not where I live, you know what I'm saying?"

"I do," said Matthew. "I do know what you're saying. I don't think it's where I live, either. My problem is that for most of my life I've been around people who tell me it *has* to be where I live. I have to have this all-or-nothing belief in the Bible."

"Matthew," she said, her face serious and calm. "Can I give you some advice? Try not to worry about it. I mean that. I think you're going to be fine the way you're going, so you shouldn't worry about people telling you what to think. Like the old hymn says. Remember?" She smiled and hummed a few notes. "'Trust and obey.'"

He felt better after talking with Margaret. But he couldn't seem to silence the warring voices in his head. Sometimes, reading the Bible in a simple, child-like way, he felt the way Ben said he felt, praying the Psalms. A petition or a song of praise jumped from the text and became his own, as natural as if he'd composed the words himself. A verse he'd memorized long ago would come back to him—"Casting all your care upon him," "Come unto me, all ye that labor"—and he'd shelter within its comforting walls, remembering Margaret's keep-it-real advice. But other times when he was reading, absorbed by a passage, a familiar phrase would set off some jangling melody he'd sung a thousand times in Sunday school or at camp. The stately cadence of the words would be drowned out by a flailing guitar he'd heard at countless high school and college gatherings. He tried to banish the tune, leaving only the words, but still the jarring music played. He read on savagely, furious with these echoes from his past, telling himself it *wasn't* the Word of God, it wasn't, it was a book to read and think about like any other, so shut up, shut up, *shut up*! Then he'd hear Will quoting sadly, one blameless finger upraised, "Blessed is the man that walketh not in the counsel of the ungodly, nor standeth in the way of sinners, nor sitteth in the seat of the scornful."

For the last few years he'd been reading the Revised Standard Version. He'd bought a copy because people at Steadfast Rock disapproved of it. Although he relished the ordinary binding and neutral appearance of his Bible, and marked his place with a leaflet quoting Oscar Romero, he still kept it easily within reach, on a lower shelf of his nightstand. If Ann noticed, she made no comment. She owned an *Oxford Annotated Bible* and a *Book of Common Prayer*, both shelved next to *Roget's Thesaurus* and her collection of cookbooks. If she came upon him reading his Bible, she smiled politely and tiptoed past as though she'd caught him looking at something nasty.

When he was growing up, and at college, people called it "devotions" or "daily quiet time." Matthew now thought of it simply as reading the Bible. Even before he got to know Ben he'd grown suspicious of what appeared to him a uniquely Protestant sacrament—one that a lot of people took more seriously than the real ones. He'd exchanged this solemn daily ritual for a loose practice of casual, unscheduled reading. He liked to plop down on the sofa when the mood struck him, and read from anywhere he felt like reading that day, as much or as little as he liked. He laughed at how he used to act as though Moses and Elijah had their quiet time every morning, with their cup of coffee and their New American Standard Bible, marking their place with an inspirational laminated bookmark. And still, after he'd repudiated and mocked his former self, Ann gave him that funny look when she found him reading his Bible, as though he were some kind of hopeless fanatic.

The heat broke toward the end of August. With the windows open and a breeze riffling the pages, he opened his Bible for ten straight mornings. Birds chirped, cars honked. From the sidewalk came footsteps and fragments of talk. The city hum mingled with the ancient words and the morning stillness. It might not have been the daily routine he'd once observed, but it still felt like he was getting ready, putting on a needed strength. He found a calmness that came from outside himself.

Ben called, officially inviting him to visit in late September. "Practice will be starting up, so I'll be kind of busy," he warned. "You'll want to bring a book or two. But we'll be able to do some stuff."

"I'm treating it as a vacation," said Matthew. "It'll be great just to be someplace different."

He fit everything he needed in a small backpack, the kind a few Steadfast people had begun carrying just before he graduated, looking pretentious since everyone lived within a stone's throw of anywhere else. In the city he'd found a backpack indispensable, and he'd learned to use it for all sorts of trips. Ann watched him collect his assortment of items and distribute them into the clever compartments.

"Flashlight? Hunting knife? Bug spray?" she teased.

"More like crossword puzzles and James Michener," he replied. "I'll probably camp out in some corner of the student union."

She accompanied him to 30th Street Station on her way to campus, and they sat on one of the pew-like benches, watching people hurry through the cavernous space. The Friday morning rush had ebbed, leaving a trickle of passengers getting a head start on the weekend. Ann talked about her research and the class she was teaching—glitches in the lab, students who looked like trouble. Matthew listened with an eye on the arrivals and departures board. He had an hour-and-a-half ride, then some time to kill before Ben got free from work. Ann told him more about her class. When his train blinked up on the board, he slung his pack on one shoulder and they stood.

She kissed him and smiled. "Have a wonderful time. Tell Ben hello."

"I will and I will." He squeezed her hand and headed for the stairway.

The sendoff had seemed a bit formal. They hadn't seen much of each other lately, the way their schedules had been. It was thoughtful of her, saying hello to Ben.

As he rode north from the city, he discovered that he and Ben had picked a good time to get together and do things outside. The hills still wore the deep green of late summer, with here and there a gold burnish. The bright reds and oranges were still to come, along with the need for sweatshirts and jackets. He'd be comfortable in jeans and a long-sleeved shirt. He gazed out the window, forgetting the book in his lap, and watched woods and golden fields yield to industrial lots, which gave way in turn to long stretches of forest. Maybe the two ends of the state weren't that different after all.

When he got off at the Laurel station he could see restaurants and stores in one direction, old campus buildings in the other. He walked into town and had a quick lunch, then set a course for a white cupola that rose above the trees. Soon he'd joined a stream of backpack-carrying people who were close to his own age. The cupola turned out to be the main administration building. Following signs and a friendly student's directions, he made his way to the student union, a modern steel-and-glass structure that reminded him of Steadfast's, except that it was three times larger. He and Ben were supposed to meet near a statue of a dog. You couldn't miss it, Ben had said.

It didn't sound like a very restful spot to sit and wait. Matthew imagined a campus landmark and meeting place, packed with noisy milling students. But after searching for fifteen minutes he could find no dog, and decided to ask for directions again. A young woman at the front desk led him around a corner, then around a sharper corner, and pointed to a recess partly concealed by large sprawling plants. In this nook sat a life-size Scottish terrier in bronze. A plaque explained that the dog, a campus mascot of sorts, had been the beloved pet of a former president of the university. Surrounding "Bunky" were four comfortable chairs flanked by tables and lamps. The cozy shrine was the perfect place for a weary guest to sit and read. Good job, Ben.

After Matthew had read for twenty minutes, a middle-aged woman in a blue pantsuit pushed a cleaning cart around the corner, and began dusting the plants and straightening the chairs. Pausing in front of Bunky, she tickled his nose with her duster.

"You'll make him sneeze," said Matthew.

The woman stuck the duster in a side pocket of the cart. "I wish I could say it brings good luck," she said, emptying a wastebasket. "But after thirty years I can't say I've noticed anything."

"What about Bunky's owner? Did *he* ever get a statue?"

She raised a forearm and pushed back a strand of gray hair. "Now that's a good question. I have no idea." She looked him over. "Are you a visitor?"

Matthew nodded.

"Well you sure picked a nice weekend for it. Prospective student, are you?"

"Just visiting a friend." For some reason he added, "One of the wrestling coaches."

She grew interested. "Which one?"

"Ben Cameron."

"Coach Cam!"

"You know him?"

"Not to talk to. But everybody knows Coach Cam. He's just the sweetest guy. How do you know him?"

"It's a long story. We went to high school together."

She nodded, apparently not very interested in the long story. "I hope you have a wonderful time here," she said. "I've been around Laurel all my life. It's a great old town."

Matthew thanked her and watched her push the squeaking cart away. He returned to his book. Now and then he looked up to watch some passing students. Through a nearby window the afternoon light slanted more and more sharply, streaking the carpet. After another hour or so he sensed a presence beyond his book. Ben stood before him, wearing a fancy dark-green Laurel warmup suit. He carried a big gym bag like the one he used in high school.

"Go ahead and get to a good stopping place," he said.

Matthew struggled to get out of the deep chair, and Ben hauled him up with a strong handclasp. For a few seconds they stood there shaking hands.

"How was practice?" Matthew asked. "You didn't have to rush over here without changing."

"I did change," said Ben. He glanced down at his new-looking jacket and pants. "Oh, these. I'm sort of expected to wear stuff like this on campus. It's a round-the-clock kind of job, I guess. Got to keep up the image all the time."

"Coach Cam."

Ben gave him a startled glance. "Where'd you hear that?"

"Cleaning lady. About an hour ago. She's a huge fan."

"Really?" Ben seemed pleased. "That's nice to know."

They made their way out of the building. Matthew watched the surge of oncoming students for grins and double-takes as they recognized Ben, but no one gave a sign. Playing it cool, perhaps, or maybe the coach was so familiar that no one gave him a second glance.

"I thought we'd stop by the house before getting dinner somewhere," said Ben.

They passed over bustling walks to an impressive field house, rising behind a grove of tall oaks. Ben skirted the main entrance and led the way to a side parking area, with signs marking each owner's space. He unlocked a sporty new Toyota, and Matthew sank down into the passenger's seat. When Ben turned the key, a blast of heavy metal shook the car. Matthew jumped.

"You were expecting 'How Great Thou Art'?" Ben laughed, switching the music off.

"How do you even know that song?" asked Matthew. "'How Great Thou Art,' I mean. You haven't sung it in church, have you?"

Ben considered. "I don't think so. I just heard it somewhere, I guess. I get records from the library, all kinds of stuff. I'm still trying to catch up."

"Hear anything good?"

Ben grimaced and shook his head.

"Well," Matthew said, "there's always Bach and Handel, I guess. Or Luther."

"Yeah. Or maybe Dylan will get born again. Again."

Ben had pulled away from the field house, and nosed slowly past the pedestrians and bicyclists. They left the campus behind, passing two- and three-story houses on tree-shaded streets. "Faculty," said Ben. After another mile or two they entered an old suburb with vegetable gardens and sagging detached garages. Men on lawn tractors crossed the big yards. One of them waved. At a house slightly smaller than the one Matthew grew up in, Ben parked in a weedy driveway.

"Just like I pictured it," said Matthew.

"Good old 3528 Tarragon Road."

Ben unlocked the heavy wooden front door. It stuck, then opened with a bang. In the silent entryway, cluttered with bagged newspapers and milk jugs, Matthew looked around and said, "No dog or cat to keep you company?"

"I'm on the road too much."

Ben went to the kitchen for some beers. From the living room, Matthew glanced into a small room across the hall. "Whoa," he said softly. He walked over for a closer look. "Oh, please," Ben protested, returning to the living room. Matthew stood looking at the collection of trophies filling several tables and a glassed-in case. High school, college, coaching. Individual championships, most valuable, most improved, team captain, "highest expression of the wrestling spirit." Cups and bowls. Tapering pedestals with tiny grapplers on top. Glittering crystal, shiny plaques. A mounted warmup jacket covered with signatures, presented to "Coach Cam." Matthew bent to read the inscriptions on the trophies. Two or three awards he remembered hearing about. The rest blurred into a picture of triumph and adulation. It was so much more than he'd imagined from Ben's vague reports and his own fleeting impressions. He turned to find Ben leaning in the doorway, picking at the label on his beer.

"I really didn't bring you here to see that."

"I know," said Matthew.

They sat down and raised their bottles in a silent toast. The living room contained nothing having to do with wrestling or athletics. Tacked to the walls were a travel poster, a Picasso print, and a reproduction of an old circus ad. A small framed photograph rested on the coffee table, showing an attractive woman in a dark-green canoe.

"Who's that?" asked Matthew, pointing to the photo.

Ben smiled. "Her name's Lisa. And I think that's all I'll say about her, except that she makes the room look better, in my opinion."

"I agree," said Matthew.

After he'd passed along Ann's good wishes, and Ben had asked about Margaret and her family, Matthew nodded toward the smaller room. "I think I'm still trying to process all of that," he said. "It's a lot."

"You have to keep that stuff somewhere," said Ben.

"I'm not saying it's showing off, or anything like that. Just the opposite. A lot of people would probably make a much bigger deal of it. I guess I just didn't realize how much success you've had—which is dumb, considering that you're Coach Cam and everything. I'm very impressed."

"Thanks," Ben said. He glanced briefly at the gleaming display. "Wrestling's a funny sport," he said. "If you go to college and you're good at football or baseball or basketball, you think about going pro. You think about it a long time before college, obviously. But wrestling's different. One or two guys might go to the Olympics, but other than that, once you graduate, there's pretty much just coaching." He shrugged. "When you look at what's available, I'm doing okay."

"You make it sound like a letdown. To me it looks like you're doing great."

"Oh, I know I'm lucky. Blessed," Ben amended with a smile. "But coaching isn't the same as wrestling. Look, if I was a football player I'd be in my prime right now. Sometimes you miss the real, player-to-player competition. The action."

Matthew looked him in the eye and said in a deadpan voice, "Don't get any ideas."

It took Ben a second or two. Then he exploded in laughter, almost spilling his beer. "I forgot! Our famous meeting on the mat!"

"How could you forget?" Matthew asked in an injured voice.

"You're right. How *could* I forget?"

"I would think it would stand out as a landmark in your career," said Matthew. "I mean, it's not like you've done much of anything else since then, right? Like wrestled hundreds of matches in all kinds of places, in front of thousands of people."

"No, seriously," said Ben. "I really do remember that time. You gave me a battle."

"I had no idea what I was doing."

"Of course you didn't. You were sloppy and you had no technique whatsoever. But you hung in there anyway. I respected that."

"I don't know what it was," said Matthew. "I guess I just didn't want to give up."

"I could tell. I didn't want to give up either. Of course I knew I would win," he said in a matter-of-fact voice, "but it turned out to be a lot harder than I expected."

"I don't know what it was," Matthew repeated.

Ben looked at him steadily for a moment. "Well, whatever it was," he said, "I hope you've still got it."

When they'd talked a little longer and finished their beers, Ben said he would change into his "civvies." He disappeared and returned in jeans and a casual buttoned shirt. They drove back into the campus neighborhood, where they ate at a Chinese restaurant—a *real* Chinese restaurant, Ben called it. He ordered knowledgeably, and they lingered over an excellent meal.

"And now I'll take you to the place you'll call home while you're in Laurel," said Ben.

Matthew had been wondering where he would stay, ever since Ben mentioned on a phone call that he would "arrange something." Ben parked on the street in front of an elegant old house with a spacious porch and stone slate-roofed turrets. The lawn looked as smooth as a golf course, dotted with shrubs and trees. Beside the broad porch stairs, tucked among sculpted yews, a sign said "Amos J. Patterson Guest House."

Matthew got out of the car, shouldering his backpack. "Looks pretty fancy," he said. "Is this another coaching perk?"

"Just a place the university runs," said Ben. "I thought it would be convenient."

The guest house was a five-minute walk from the field house, where Ben had practice the next morning. They could meet there at lunchtime and have the rest of the day free. After Ben, brusquely waving Matthew away, dealt with check-in and left for the night, Matthew followed the desk clerk's directions through a lobby and up a carpeted stairway. He found his room on the second floor, and stood motionless as the door clicked shut behind him. The place looked like a first-class hotel. The bed, chairs, and tables all possessed real character, solid and substantial in gleaming walnut and oak. Matthew walked to the nightstand, pulled a silent gliding drawer, and looked down. You had to hand it to those guys. He picked up the glossy new Bible and sat on the bed.

It seemed like days since he'd kissed Ann goodbye at the station. He'd really needed to get out of town. He kicked off his shoes, swung his feet onto the bed, and settled back against the headboard. Without intending to he read all of the Letter to the Philippians, then James and parts of Hebrews. He didn't try to absorb any special lesson, just went with the flow, following the writers' meandering train of thought. Then he read another chapter of Michener. He thought about watching the news, just to see what Philadelphia looked like from out here, but ended up leaving the remote untouched. Through the open window came the click and whirr of insects, and an abrupt screeching that might have been an owl. He got ready for bed, and lay thinking and praying for a few minutes before sleeping through the night. He woke a little after seven o'clock to mild sunshine.

Downstairs, the woman at the desk told him which campus buildings would be open, and recommended some sights to see. He walked into town for a leisurely breakfast, then explored for an hour, savoring the lazy Saturday-morning quiet. He discovered a few more hideaways like Bunky's, and winding staircases that led to ornate, parlor-like lounges. In the library he visited the periodicals department, feeling the ghost of a professional interest. All morning he asked himself what might have happened if he'd transferred from Steadfast to a place like this, instead of spending four years with his mind on a leash. Then he thought about how much he liked his job, and about Ann and Margaret and Ben, and decided things had worked out all right.

By midday he knew his way around like any student, and walked to the field house in a couple of minutes. Inside, at the end of a dim hallway, he heard male voices. He stopped at an office where Ben stood talking with two men, both with the same compact wrestler's build and the same close-cropped hair. Ben introduced him to the head coach, Van Watson, and to his fellow assistant Nicky Gervais. Matthew had expected the coach to be a grizzled, fatherly sort, but Watson couldn't have been older than thirty-five. Nicky Gervais was Matthew's age or younger.

"This is it, Matthew," said Coach Watson. "The brain trust of Laurel wrestling."

Matthew couldn't think of a reply.

"Matthew isn't really a wrestling fan," Ben told his colleagues. "We know each other from school."

"You're from Stanton?" asked Gervais.

Matthew nodded. "Originally. I live in Philadelphia now."

"I'm from the Pittsburgh area too—Aliquippa," the assistant said. "Ben and I try to keep these East Coast assholes in line."

"Sometimes I think I might turn into one of those East Coast assholes myself," said Matthew.

"Nah," said Gervais. "You're from western P-A, man. You're a good guy for life."

"He actually believes that," Ben said to Matthew.

Gervais drew a business card from his shirt pocket. "Here, take this," he said to Matthew. "In case you ever need someone to ride over with, or to hang out with there. I like to keep up my area connections."

"Thanks," said Matthew, tucking the card in his wallet.

"What I know about these western P-A guys," said Coach Watson, "is they can run a decent wrestling squad."

Ben picked up his gym bag, and he and Matthew left the office. When they were outside, Ben said, "Coach can be a bit much. Nicky's all right, though."

They got into Ben's car and drove away from campus, picking up sandwiches and sodas at a deli. It was another warm sunny day, with plenty of afternoon left. In a few minutes the houses were spaced further apart than in Ben's neighborhood. In a few minutes more they saw no houses at all. They climbed gradually into a wild, overgrown area, with dense thickets crowding the shoulder and sunlight flashing through trees. Ben turned onto a smaller road when they reached a state park sign. They crept along narrow twisting pavement that tunneled into older, taller woods. Through their open windows they heard the engine echo in the dimness. The air felt cool and damp. Suddenly sunshine cascaded through an opening, where Ben parked in a small gravel lot. They got out and stood craning their necks, looking up at a ring of canopy traversed by darting, singing birds.

"There's a nice trail over there," said Ben, his voice loud, pointing. "It takes two or three hours, depending how fast you walk."

"Perfect," said Matthew. He hoisted the bag with their lunch. "And we'll eat soon?"

"Don't worry. There's a good place not too far."

Matthew couldn't see where the trail began. Ben parted some branches to reveal a narrow path. They struck out at a medium pace, ascending across bulging roots and slick rocks to a ridge that ran alongside a forty-foot drop. From below they heard passing cars, but soon the ridge curved away, leaving only the chickadees' whirring calls. The trail veered and climbed, up a steep slope with dug-in timbers to help with footing. Matthew fell behind, and Ben stopped to wait. They continued more slowly. Matthew had always thought he got plenty of exercise in the city, walking as much as he did, but scaling a hill was different. Ben pulled ahead of him again, and again halted.

"Take your time," he called back.

"It isn't just the climb," said Matthew. "I'm not used to being around someone who's in shape like you."

"Sorry."

"I'm okay. Just give me a second."

He stopped and puffed, waiting for his breath to return and his heart to calm down. What must it be like, he wondered, to inhabit a body that always did what you wanted it to do? Did you feel invincible, or did it just get to be routine? When they were younger, Ben had kept in shape as a matter of course—had in fact gone far beyond merely "in shape," fine-tuning his weight like a radio dial, building an endurance to outlast any opponent's. Now, robbed of his sport, he stayed fit through sheer force of habit. In all but the daily contests on the mat, Ben remained a wrestler.

The trail leveled off at a cluster of towering rocks. Candy wrappers, bottles, and orange rinds littered the ground. It was obviously a popular stopping point. Ben and Matthew sat down and ate their sandwiches, their backs against a lichened boulder. Other hikers entered the clearing, nodded, kept climbing. For several minutes Matthew tipped his head back and closed his eyes. If he'd been alone he might have slept.

From the rocks the trail rose even more steeply, but Matthew felt better after food and a rest. They paced themselves for ten or fifteen minutes, until Ben stopped and pointed into unbroken woods. "Here's where we head over to my spot," he said.

"What spot?"

"You'll see."

He left the trail and pushed his way through saplings and brambles. Matthew followed. Limbs whipped their arms and faces. Fallen branches dragged at their feet. At least the ground here was even, part of a broad hilltop or plateau. After an interval of slow progress, at times closing their eyes against poking branches, they saw blue sky ahead through the screen of leaves. Soon they stood on a small outcrop, looking down across rocks and ravines to treetops that stretched for miles under a pristine sky.

"How did you find this place?" asked Matthew, admiring the view.

Ben shrugged. "Partly a hunch, partly luck. I don't think very many people know about it."

They sat and gazed at the swells of forest and the blue-green horizon. No sound reached them from the distant floor, or from the woods at their backs. Yellow and orange tipped the foliage in patches, more color than Matthew had observed from the train. Here and there a crease cut between the treetops, perhaps a creek bed or an abandoned road. A breeze fluttered the nearby leaves, and disturbed the surface below.

"How often have you been here?" asked Matthew.

"Ten times or so. Maybe more."

"Is this where you pray?"

"Now and then. Or I just sit and be with God."

Matthew thought about that. The wind rustled in his ears.

"It's like we've said before," said Ben. "Sometimes you want to get away from all the words."

"What words, exactly?"

Ben ducked his head. His hair covered his eyes. "Church words, to begin with."

"What about Bible words, like the Psalms?"

"They're okay. Mountains and seas. Lists of animals. All that. Out here, though, it's *direct*, you know? I don't *need* the words. I feel like I'm sitting with the one who made all this. I can tell he's around me, wanting me to take it in."

Matthew raised his eyes to the misty horizon, the dim gradations where forest merged with sky. The towering cumuli made him visualize taller mountains, *real* mountains, rising jagged, snow-capped, obscured by clouds. He imagined a dark ocean rolling, full of life. He imagined the blue sky before him at night, strewn with stars. He felt the roaring vastness of the created world.

"It's not like I have some unusual craving. Everyone says they want to get beyond the words," said Ben. He turned, lips curled in a rueful smile. "Seems like mostly they just come up with more words."

"More songs."

"Yeah," Ben laughed. "More songs. Till you can't hear yourself think. Let alone hear the Word of God."

"Do you think you can hear the Word of God out here?"

Ben nodded. "Yeah. I do."

"What does it say?"

Ben looked out over the forest. "I don't know," he said. "I don't know if it's saying anything. God spoke the Word and the world came forth. When I look at the world now, I can hear the Word still. It resonates in creation, doesn't it? So I don't hear what the Word says. I hear what it did, and what it does."

Matthew started to ask another question, then stopped himself. He listened to the wind, and watched the colors change with the lengthening afternoon. They sat for another half hour, saying little. When they got to their feet they stretched, and massaged muscles numbed by sitting on the rocks. They started walking again.

Shortly after they'd fought through the brush and rejoined the trail, it looped back down in the direction from which they'd come. They strode quickly, helped by the downhill grade, startling a deer and overtaking more hikers. They reached the parking area as daylight began to fade. Ben suggested a pizza at his favorite place, where Matthew found that the exercise and fresh air had made him hungrier than he thought.

Ben dropped him off at the guest house. Unsure whether he was kidding or not, Matthew asked, "Are we going to church tomorrow?"

Ben's eyes got a hunted look. "Sunday's my one chance to sleep in," he said, "what with practice and everything. To be honest, I could use the rest. I thought we'd do some stuff in the afternoon, then I'll fix us some dinner at my place."

"Sounds good," said Matthew.

They decided that Ben would pick him up at noon, the guest house checkout time. Matthew settled down for another quiet night with the Gideons and Michener. In the morning he thought about going to church by himself, but discovered, when it came to selecting one, that he felt no less wary than Ben. He sat by his window and read Colossians. That afternoon

Ben showed him some out-of-the-way corners of campus, and they spent an hour in the university museum.

At Ben's they worked together preparing a big meal. Matthew stood on the back deck and sipped a beer, poking at their steaks while Ben started a salad inside. The day glided toward a peaceful close. Rabbits nibbled at the overgrown lawn. Swallows dipped and veered. Two houses away, a woman took down sheets from a clothesline, cramming the billowy masses into a small basket. Matthew thought about the visit, how he'd traveled to this ordinary, unexciting place to spend time with a college wrestling coach. He'd lost touch with most of his other friends. At St. Sebastian's no one talked about anything important. He liked Margaret, but she was a work friend, and his boss at that. Somehow Ben was different from all of those others. He still seemed a miracle, calling Matthew's name from the library stairs, announcing that he'd "turned Christian." No one else talked about God the way Ben did. No one else required of Matthew the same honesty, the same pursuit of something real. He looked up from the grill at a filmy half-moon, just visible in the glowing sky. He wondered absently if Ben needed him the way that he needed Ben.

They ate outside at a half-size picnic table, a relic from Ben's Stanton childhood. Matthew asked about the wrestling season. He learned about weight classes and certifying procedures. He learned about dual meets, multiple duals, and tournaments. He remembered Nicky Gervais's card, took it from his wallet, and examined the printed phrases.

"What exactly does 'Wrestling Associate' mean?"

"It means he's an assistant coach like me," said Ben. "Nicky's a little funny that way, into titles and stuff. He doesn't take it too seriously, though."

"Do you have some cards like this?"

"I probably have some around somewhere. They come with the job, like those Laurel things I had on when I met you at the union."

Matthew thought about the drab New Prospects office. There was letterhead printed with an uninspired logo, but that was about it. The job had never offered those extra little touches that turned showing up for work into an occasion. "Must be kind of nice, all these fancy perks like the business cards and clothes," he said. "Makes you feel like you're somebody."

Ben looked away, out toward the scruffy lawn. "It's all just wrestling, really. Guys who are any good, that's all they're in it for. You can't get caught up in those other things. Most of the time it's like they aren't even there."

"Other things" meant the crowds, the media, the uniforms, the equipment—all the things that Matthew had always assumed were the point of playing a varsity sport. For Ben, none of that had mattered. He'd only been in it for the wrestling. Even the trophies and awards were nothing but mementos, reminders of an experience that Ben would never have again. It didn't seem fair.

Toward dusk Matthew said he'd like to get to the station. They arrived a half hour before his train. Matthew apologized, and said Ben must have things to do, but Ben insisted he'd wait with him. They found a bench on the deserted platform, and sat down with Matthew's backpack slumped between them. It occurred to Matthew that he could have bought a souvenir or two as he wandered around campus, maybe something for Ann from the bookstore. Then he realized he wouldn't have known what to get her. He couldn't imagine giving Ann a Laurel mug, or a stuffed creature waving a pennant. He thought of flowers—but you bought flowers to welcome someone home, not to bring home from a trip. He wondered whether Ann would be waiting for him at 30th Street. He couldn't remember whether he'd told her when his train got back.

At the other end of the bench Ben sat, ankle propped on a knee, fingers laced behind his head. He seemed to be absorbing the last soft light. Matthew drew a deep slow breath. Down in his bones he knew this silence, these empty streets, this sense of peace and fulfillment. Sunday evening. Even on a day when he hadn't been to church, it felt different from other times: the winding down of a day of worship and rest, the expectant lull before the work week.

"Sunday evenings can make me nostalgic," he said. "It's from all those services when I was a kid. Afterward you'd come outside, and it would be twilight just like this. Quiet and peaceful and content. You'd go home and have whatever you wanted for supper, because you'd already had your big Sunday dinner. There was this feeling of enjoying the last bit of weekend, before you went back to school."

"Did you mind it? Having to go to church twice in a day?"

"Yes and no. Of course I missed some baseball games, and just goofing around with kids in the neighborhood. I missed some shows on TV. Sometimes I felt like a freak, or like I was deprived compared to other people. Other times it felt like this. A sort of blessed feeling. A good way to end the day."

"I can imagine it," Ben said, nodding. "It would be kind of nice." He sat forward, looking across the tracks and away into the mild light. "I don't know anyone else who had experiences like that, who would talk about them the way you do. I like to think about what it would be like, hanging around with people who believe the same way." He turned toward Matthew. "Maybe someday, you know? Someday when I'm ready."

"Sure," said Matthew. "When you're ready."

"Thanks for coming," said Ben. "It means a lot to me."

"Thanks for having me." They sat in silence for a minute in the gathering dusk. "There's something I've wondered about," said Matthew. "How exactly did you come to believe? You didn't say much about it, that day in the Steadfast library."

After a few moments Ben answered, speaking slowly but without hesitation. "My first year wrestling in college, I got on a pretty long winning streak. People noticed, and it was fun. I definitely enjoyed the success. After a while, though, it didn't feel good anymore. I had to psych myself up for each match, trying to feel confident when really I was fighting down my fear that this would be the match when I finally lost. I felt miserable, trying to call up some kind of strength in myself and wondering if this would be the time it ran out.

"When I did lose, it was just an ordinary match, not a big tournament or anything. The guy had a good day, and I made some mistakes. I got away from campus as soon as I could, and sat on a bench in a park." He laughed softly. "Like any other loser, right? I sat there intending to feel worthless and crappy until the feeling went away. Except I didn't feel crappy. I started to feel good."

"The pressure was off," said Matthew. "It must have been a huge relief."

Ben shook his head. "That wasn't it. It wasn't just that I got the loss over with, like getting a shot when you're a kid, or taking a big test. I didn't just feel relieved, I felt happy. All through the streak, I'd had to count on myself. I had to make myself perform at a high enough level to win. When I lost, I thought I'd feel terrible about myself, or even despair, but I didn't. I sat on that bench and I started to see myself in a different way—or at least, I don't know, I got a glimpse of a different way. Instead of depending entirely on myself, and worrying about whether I had what it took to succeed, I could be okay because of something or someone else. For the first time in my life, I could imagine trusting in someone besides myself."

Matthew waited a little longer, then asked, "So that was how you became a Christian? You started trusting in God then?"

"I think becoming a Christian came later. First I just had to discover a belief in God, a sense of meaning from God. But yeah, that moment on the bench was the beginning. And when I think about why I believe in Christ *now*, it isn't because of things I've read in the Bible, or some process of reasoning I went through. It's because of the time I experienced losing and then realized I could still matter to God. That's my story that I always go back to. I believe because of that story."

A few minutes later the train slid in, and they got to their feet. They watched the lighted chambers ease to a halt. "Seeya," they told each other, shaking hands.

Matthew found a seat and looked out the window. Ben stood on the platform, gazing at the sky. As the train pulled away he still stood there motionless, hands in his pockets, head tilted back. Matthew watched him dwindle and disappear, then watched the town dissolve into nondescript lots, empty roads, dry cornfields. He thought about having a story, what that would mean. He didn't know if he had a story. What did *that* mean, if he didn't have one? Darkness fell, interrupted by the lonely lights at intersections and taverns. He read for a while, dozed, read some more.

It was almost ten by the time he reached the apartment. From the street it appeared to be unlit—a little careless on Ann's part, but no big deal. He unlocked their door and reached for the floor lamp. His hand groped in empty space. He took a few steps and switched on a table lamp. A different living room materialized, with strange gaps and newly glaring surfaces, patches of floor and wall he shouldn't be able to see. Half the furniture was gone. He rushed to the bedroom. No bed. In the kitchen the toaster was missing. A gray fluff of dust and crumbs lay where the microwave used to be. He returned to the living room. The TV and stereo were in their usual places, but Ann's new computer, her pride and joy, was gone. In its place he found a note in her small precise hand.

Dear Matthew,

I hope you had a nice visit with Ben.

Moving out like this seemed easier for both of us. We obviously had no future together, so I decided on my own to take the initiative, and make the break as quickly and neatly as I could. You're so much deeper and more serious than I am, Matthew. I was keeping you tied to the surface.

I tried to remember what was whose. Please let me know if I made any mistakes. I'm staying with Ron and Judy for now, but will continue to pay my share of the rent until the lease is up. That seems fair.

I hope things won't feel too awkward at church!

Ann

He sank down on the sofa and read the note several times. Should he find fault with what she'd written, what she'd done? She made her decision sound so simple and logical, he sat there half-believing that everything was normal. He was overreacting to feel shocked and betrayed. Maybe people did things like this all the time. Where he'd gone wrong, as she generously suggested, was in getting involved with someone like her in the first place. Now he could start his Philadelphia life over again, true to himself and his own way of doing things. But it was an empty, depressing way to begin, he thought, looking at the desolate room.

He got up and started moving furniture around, trying to disguise the gaps. Ann was right, there was no need for drama. Just rearrange what's left and get on with it. There hadn't been much between them anyway. *I hope things won't feel too awkward at church!* That one chirpy line kept making him laugh. How exactly *does* one act, bumping into one's ex-lover in the house of the Lord? What would be the smooth, correct way to do that? He kept laughing as he pushed the sofa and chairs back and forth. Then he yanked out the folding bed from the sofa, found a blanket in a closet, and slept.

He didn't return to St. Sebastian's right away—not because he wanted to avoid Ann, but to protect and preserve his new life. He replaced almost nothing she'd taken, except for buying a five-dollar toaster on Market Street, and a few pots and pans in a thrift store. Gradually, the half-furnished apartment spoke to him of freedom and new beginnings. After work he opened the windows, something Ann never did, and let in the fresh October air. He read the Bible when he felt like it, without worrying about whether he looked pious. On weekends he ate and slept at irregular times. He tried new restaurants and stores. He explored whole blocks and neighborhoods that he and Ann had neglected on their walks.

He asked himself what he really needed, and discovered that the answer was "Not much." It became a game, paring back possessions and habits. The can of air freshener went first, thanks to the open windows. He drank his coffee black, without the flavored creamers Ann liked. He gave away a half-dozen expensive liqueurs she left behind. He quit buying dryer sheets. He quit buying conditioner for his hair. He quit buying *TV Guide*. He let the *New York Times* subscription run out, and made do with the *Inquirer*. He threw away the polishes, waxes, disinfectants, and deodorizers that Ann had thought cleaning required, and went at it with a little cleanser and some liquid oil soap.

At work he flirted with Laura. He made a bigger deal of the cookies and pies she brought from Cherry Hill, and they had lunch a few times, quick meals they picked up from a food truck and carried to a nearby park. They talked about the Phillies and had long debates about why "MASH" wasn't good anymore. If Ann thought he was too serious, too wrapped up in theology, then she should have seen him listen while Laura explained why "Dynasty" was superior to "Dallas." In Laura he finally found someone who shared at least some of his tastes in music. She listened to Ultravox and the Human League, while Matthew was more the Mission of Burma, Gang of Four type, but each always knew any band the other named. He thought about asking her to go to a Center City club, but it seemed too much like a date, and a date might ruin everything. No more Patty LeFleurs, he'd long since promised himself.

On one of the last days when they would be able to eat outside, they split a hoagie while sitting on a bench in Rittenhouse Square. Laura looked sharp in a bright red woolen jacket. Matthew had on his navy blue Steadfast Rock windbreaker.

She tugged his jacket sleeve. "Hey. When you go to church, do you keep your coat on in the pew?"

"No," said Matthew. He'd never heard of such a thing. "Why?"

"We always do. Yesterday when we went to Mass, they'd put coat racks near the entrance, so of course we all walked right past them. Coat racks! They just looked so totally out of place, you know? My mom turned to me and said, 'What are we, Protestant?'"

Matthew laughed. "So much for ecumenical progress."

"Well, come on," said Laura. "You can't force these things. At least give people a little warning."

As Thanksgiving approached, Matthew decided he would stay in Philadelphia and then go home to Stanton at Christmas. St. Sebastian's always needed volunteers for their annual free Thanksgiving dinner. If he could slip into the serving line without anyone noticing, it might be a good way to break the ice.

The Reagan homeless were everywhere—old men in overcoats trudging through the August heat, slippered women pulling carts piled high with junk. Laura referred to them as "bag ladies" and "street people," getting The Eyebrow from Margaret. New Prospects dealt exclusively with employment, referring the homeless to other agencies, so this crisis hadn't hit Matthew where he worked. The down and out, the addicted, and the mentally ill lived for the most part in a different world; but Matthew, with a surge of his old college idealism, felt he needed to do his part in the new struggle. On Thanksgiving morning he walked the familiar four blocks to the church.

The basement fellowship room was crowded with long rows of tables. From the kitchen came voices, laughter, the clash of pots and pans. He looked in and found ten or so people, some carrying dishes back and forth and doing things with turkeys, while others poured, stirred, and chopped. Ann, her hair in a kerchief, scrubbed potatoes at a sink.

"Hi Matthew!" she called, as though she'd seen him the day before. "Peel this!" She threw him a potato, which he managed to neatly catch.

"Maybe I'd better wash my hands," he said.

She made room for him at the sink, and in seconds they were peeling, cooking, and mashing, pretending to resume a home life they'd never had. Fake as it was, it got them through the moment. From the big room outside the kitchen they began to hear shuffling footsteps, scraping chairs, noisy coughing.

"Show time!" said a woman at the stove.

For the next half hour Matthew stood behind the serving tables, dropping a scoop of mashed potatoes, squashing a well, spooning gravy, passing the plate, taking another. Across the table he watched a procession of waiting hands, most of them grimy and wrinkled. He looked up now and then at expressionless faces, or eyes fixed intently on the plate he held, or a small nod, a murmur of thanks. "You're welcome," he said. After Pastor Jill had said a prayer and people began to eat, Matthew loaded a plate of his own and squeezed in at the end of a table.

A hundred shaggy heads and woolen caps bent over the food. Except for the clink of cutlery the room was nearly silent. Over the crowd hung a heavy odor of food and unwashed bodies. Chewing a mouthful of salty turkey, Matthew glanced at the dark-skinned man beside him.

"How's it going?" he said.

The man paused in his eating, turned with questioning eyes, and said nothing.

"You doing all right in this colder weather?"

"I like it better than the heat."

"Good," said Matthew, nodding. "That's good. Let's hope winter isn't too bad."

"We can hope." The man went back to his meal.

During cleanup, Matthew found Ann at the opposite end of a table he helped carry to the storage room. The line of helpers stalled while someone up front straightened the tables, and he and Ann stopped for a moment in the dim hall. Ann's eyes met his. She offered a timid smile.

"Is everything . . .?" she said. "Are we . . .?"

"Everything's fine," said Matthew, trying to make the curt reply sound a little less unfriendly. He felt nothing—certainly no interest in a long conversation. "Thanks for helping with the rent."

She shrugged. "Well."

"How are you?" he said. "How's work?"

"Same. You?"

"Same."

They smiled. She was a decent enough person, he supposed. He just wanted to leave.

"I'll probably see you around," he said. "I haven't decided yet how much I'll be coming here."

"I understand," she said, which for some reason, for the first time, he found irritating. "How's Ben?"

"Busy. You know, with the season and everything."

They picked up the table and carried it into the storage room, where they leaned it with elaborate care against the others. Matthew looked over at her where she straightened, dusting her hands. He smiled and gave a little wave. Then he walked down the hall and climbed the stairs from the basement.

A few days later he called Ben to find out his plans for Christmas. He thought they might drive over to Stanton together.

"Can't do it, bro. I'll be stuck here. There's this big tournament coming up."

"I figured," said Matthew. "Well, good luck."

"Thanks. Thanks for calling."

Each year Matthew received a handful of Christmas cards from grandparents, uncles, and aunts. He got one from Margaret, and from two or three Steadfast friends he could barely remember. He hadn't begun sending cards himself, knowing once he started he'd be obliged to keep it up. This year he received a handmade card from Ben. The front bore a blazing white star against a black background. Inside, in small black script, appeared the single word "Emmanuel." The card was signed "Ben."

A fairly long letter was enclosed. Propping the card beside his reading lamp, Matthew settled down to the letter, which read in part:

I've been thinking about your nostalgia for evening church, and whether I should try to find a church of my own. The idea makes me nervous. At the same time I know it might be something I need. Did you know I've never taken communion? Anywhere? I know I must be missing something.

You have to understand how hard it is to pick a church when it hasn't been a part of you all your life. Remember being a kid on the playground, how the merry-go-round with a bunch of kids on it would get going fast, like a blur, and you'd stand there wishing you could ride? You'd want to get on really bad, and you'd watch for your chance, maybe a hand from one of the other kids. But no one ever offered a hand or made room for you, and the metal bars flew past and banged your hand when you reached for them, and it seemed like you could never jump on.

That's what starting to go to church feels like to me. I can't find an opening, some way to begin. I think if I try, I'll end up on my ass, scraped and bruised. It's scary, man! Way scarier than a match in front of hundreds of people, if you can believe that. I've changed a lot over the last few years, so maybe I'll change about this. Something might come up that shows me the way. I need to have faith that that could happen. In the meantime, I plan to keep meeting God on my own.

Two days before Christmas, Matthew packed a few things, collected the gifts he'd bought for his family, and locked the apartment. Nothing more than a bill or two would come in the mail. The plants had all disappeared with Ann. He caught the train for Pittsburgh at 30th Street Station, and settled down for the long ride across the state. He'd done it before. He barely glanced at the gray woods crawling past the window.

This would be his third trip home since moving to Philadelphia. During his Steadfast years, with Stanton barely an hour away, he'd visited often—to escape from campus, bring home some laundry, make his mother happy. It was easy to move between dorm life and his family. People spoke the same language, prayed the same prayers, and sang the same hymns. True, at home he lacked friends his own age, but taking a break from Steadfast friends was one of the reasons to go home. These visits from

Philadelphia, however, were another story. It wasn't so much the chasm between city life and his small home town. That was obvious, and more exhilarating than anything else, reminding himself that he'd adopted a new and more interesting way of life. Even thinking up ways to conceal—or, as he'd finally admitted was more likely, brazen out—his true relationship with Ann hadn't been too nerve-wracking, merely a matter of holding his breath when her name came up and hurrying on to some other topic. And now, of course, she'd become one less problem. What really fatigued him, and filled him with dread, was people at home thinking he was still the same person he'd been, with the same assumptions, tastes, and habits. From all the evidence he provided, why should they think anything different? He prayed before dinner when his turn came around. He piled into the car for every service. He sang "The Old Rugged Cross" with the proper conviction, and threw in a dollar when the plate went by. He never knew whether to set the record straight, or just play along and keep up the false impression. He'd changed from the Matt Lindley they'd watched grow up, the Matt whom everyone took for granted they knew. He might have felt more like insisting on that fact, and remaining true to his real self, if he could figure out the self he'd become.

Near Altoona, when the conductor announced "the famous Horse-shoe Curve," he opened his eyes and saw in front of him, weirdly visible, the cars that trailed behind his own. It was like looking at the back of his own head. He watched the line of cars as they pushed him around the bend, imagining the passengers inside staring back while he stared at them, their gazes mingling across a gulf of air.

Several times during the long day he remembered a man he'd seen sitting against a wall in 30th Street Station, surrounded by dusty trash bags containing his belongings. He could have been very young or very old. You couldn't tell whether the gray in his hair and beard were from age or a buildup of oily dirt. Maybe he'd been at the Thanksgiving dinner at St. Sebastian's. He might even have sat at Matthew's table. How would Matthew remember him, or distinguish him from the hundreds of other slumped gray figures? His head bent forward, hiding his face. Passengers stepped around him, making a quick detour in their rush to a platform or taxi.

Volunteering at that dinner had been the right thing to do, a small way to bring help and comfort to people like the homeless man. Working at New Prospects helped as well, lending a hand to people seeking a livelihood, stability, a little dignity. Matthew thought of all the years when such needs had

95

never crossed his mind, before his dawning awareness in high school and at Steadfast. He thanked God he'd finally gotten the chance to make a little dent in the desperate needs of the city, doing work that mattered to him and that he'd prepared for. For the most part neglected by the churches he'd grown up in, this kind of service, he believed, embodied what it meant to be a Christian. Now that he was finally acting on that conviction, he should feel happy, complete, fulfilled. But he didn't. He'd ruthlessly abandoned the simple answers and thoughtless confidence of his childhood, and then the abstract systems of the Steadfast crowd. He just hadn't found something satisfying to replace all that, something besides doing good deeds. And it troubled him that he cared so much about this. Maybe Ann was right, his upbringing went deeper than he thought. Maybe he wasn't cut out for a life of helping people after all.

The short day waned. The gray mountains turned into brooding shapes, spattered with lights as the train neared Pittsburgh. Soon it rumbled past sidings and beat-up sheds that vanished as the station swallowed up the cars. After a long wait in his seat, he followed his fellow passengers off the train and up the stairs to the cramped waiting area, always a shock after the seedy grandeur of 30th Street. His sister Miriam, coat unzipped to reveal a Steadfast Rock sweatshirt, stood waving. He grinned and sliced toward her through the crowd.

"Baby sis is all grown up, picking people up at the train station!" he said, giving her a peck on a chilly pink cheek.

"Merry Christmas to you too," she said.

"Merry Christmas."

"Come on, we hafta hurry. Mom doesn't want dinner to get cold."

Miriam had parked their mother's Rabbit close by. She waited for Matthew to stow his things in the backseat and buckle up, then pulled away from the station, steering easily through rush-hour traffic. Matthew couldn't remember his sister driving him anywhere before. Her eyes flicked between the street and the rear-view mirror, hands and feet efficiently operating gear shift and clutch. In a few minutes they merged onto the expressway, headed home.

"How's sophomore year going?" he asked. She'd just completed her third semester at Steadfast.

"Not as fun as last year," she said. "A couple of my friends transferred."

Good for them, Matthew thought, but said, "That would be tough."

"Oh—Dr. Wei said to tell you hello."

"Dr. Wei? The philosophy professor?"

"No. Dr. Wei the basketball coach." She rolled her eyes.

"Are you taking 101, the course I took?"

She shook her head. "Ethics."

Of course—ethics would be the practical thing to take. Miriam was a business major, to his parents' delight. She'd looked at several colleges besides Steadfast, but decided to stick with family tradition. To the extent he still knew Miriam, he thought Steadfast must be perfect for her. In high school she'd had a big social circle, so she'd love dorm life, and the other friendships that sprang up so easily. Steadfast had its cliques and castes like anyplace else, but the shared beliefs made such sorting pretty mild. If you were excluded, it was done gently; and if you persisted, you could probably fit in anyway. Even the biggest snobs and the tightest floor buddies couldn't prevail against the official Christian unity. Miriam must feel right at home there. As a freshman she'd joined the Chapel Committee and Campus Spiritual Life Leadership. As far as Matthew knew, she'd never questioned her faith. She'd never wavered or sought something more.

They arrived home with fifteen minutes to spare, but his mother still worried that the noodles would dry out and the vegetables get cold. She laughed at herself, dried her hands, and gave him a kiss. His father took his backpack and stowed it behind the umbrella stand.

"I couldn't believe how fast Miriam got us here," said Matthew. "When did she learn to drive in Pittsburgh like that?"

"She's always been a savvy kid," his father said. "Maybe she'll turn out to be a city slicker like you."

"Oh Dad," said Miriam, heading for the bathroom.

"There are worse fates," Matthew called after her.

He let his guard down over dinner, helped by the fact that he was starving. It was one of his mother's most ordinary meals, beef stroganoff made with a can of mushroom soup, but he wolfed down two big helpings. His father had come home the day before from a business trip to Toledo, and Miriam complained about her final exam in Accounting that turned out to be different from what everyone expected. Matthew complimented his mother on the food, not wanting her to feel like the neglected homebody. She received his praise with a grateful smile. "I'm just glad to have everyone here," she said. "I love having four mouths to feed again."

On Christmas Eve they went to the candlelight service at Ebenezer. Matthew braced for an awkward, embarrassing ordeal, but the familiar ceremony brought only peace. He could still listen in wonder as Will read from Luke about the shepherds and angels. The babe in the manger was still the savior of the world. "Silent Night" was still "Silent Night." He tipped his candle toward Miriam's and watched the wick flame. Shadows quivered on the paper disk, on Miriam's hands, on the pew before him. He looked up. The whole sanctuary trembled and glowed with a holy radiance from his childhood.

The lights went on, and after a few moments the little console organ wheezed out "Joy to the World." The congregation drifted toward the door in a festive commotion, waiting to shake the pastor's hand. At the front of the line, Will seized Matthew's elbow and said, "Matt! Here you are, finally. I've been saving one special just for you. Are you ready?"

Matthew smiled and nodded.

Will's voice dropped to a radio announcer's deadpan drone. "How did the coffee shop waitress decide who she would go out with?"

"I don't know," said Matthew. "How?"

"She had a really good drip filter!"

Matthew laughed, along with several people who'd been standing in earshot. He kept on laughing as the line pushed him toward the coat racks and out the door. Behind him, Miriam and his father let out a few last chuckles. Only his mother failed to appreciate the joke, pursing her lips as though it had been in slightly poor taste. Matthew decided she must have been reluctant to lose the candlelight mood.

For the rest of the visit he kept soaking up the comforts of home, lending a hand with Christmas dinner but otherwise pitching in on the minimum of chores—as far as Miriam would let him get away with it. "You're no more a guest here than I am," she pointed out. He thought about calling some high school friends, but couldn't seem to find a good time. He watched bowl games on TV, and helped assemble a thousand-piece jigsaw puzzle of Mount Fuji, a gift from missionary friends of his parents.

He flipped through *Newsweek* and *Christianity Today* in the family room, where the commentaries and sermons frowned down, unanswerable. The cracked spines and faded dustcovers meant less to him now than his toy cars and stuffed animals in the attic, but they still projected an inescapable authority, their methods and systems unchallenged. He couldn't argue against them, he'd merely stepped around them, convinced they no longer belonged in his life. And so they would always be there.

On his last night at home the family sat around the card table, determined to conquer Mount Fuji. A section of sky and some flowers in the foreground remained. Matthew and Miriam worked on the flowers, racing to find each missing piece before the other could grab it. Their mother sat back in her chair, contemplating a blue, white, and violet piece that might belong among the flowers, but could just as easily blend into the sky. Matthew had decided he would worry about that piece later.

Gradually his mother and father lost interest, leaving Matthew and Miriam to complete the final stages. His father stood and stretched, wandered off to the kitchen, and came back munching a cookie.

"How did your talk with Virginia go?" he asked their mother, who remained seated at the table, watching Matthew and Miriam.

"Well, I was right in my hunch," she said. "She was ready to talk about spiritual things. I wasn't forcing it at all."

"That's good," said Matthew's father.

"Yes, I think so. We talked about sin and the need for forgiveness. Then I gave her some scriptures from Romans. I explained that we can know for sure that we're saved, because we have God's word on it."

"What did she say to that?" asked Matthew.

"She said she'd think about it." His mother looked at him curiously. "Why do you ask?"

"I was just wondering how she reacted to that idea about having God's word on it."

"Why?"

"Because not everyone feels the same way about the Bible."

"It's the Word of God."

"Well—but not everybody believes that. I know people who would just as soon live by their dishwasher owner's manual as by the Bible."

"That's a little sacrilegious, Matthew."

"All I'm saying is that there are people who don't believe in the Bible the way we do. To be honest, I don't know how I'd argue with them. I think you have to take the Bible on faith."

"Now that's a slippery slope," said his father, sitting down and pointing at Matthew with the rest of his cookie. "If we just take the Bible on faith, as you put it, then our belief in it is subjective, and the next thing you know we're picking and choosing parts we like or don't like, or saying we don't take certain parts literally. Faith needs to be based on the objective written Word of God."

"But how is that faith?" asked Matthew.

"Aha!" said Miriam.

She planted a finger triumphantly on the lower half of the puzzle. Matthew leaned closer to look. There was the mystery piece, its shape just recognizable among the flowers that bordered Mount Fuji.

The train ride back to Philadelphia seemed to take a long time. The last of Pittsburgh fell away and then regathered itself, like a cold that wouldn't quit. He still felt groggy from an idle New Year's Day spent eating his mother's heavy food, although of course there'd been nothing stronger to drink than ginger ale. Stuffed and pampered, he itched to be on his own again, following his own routines. With the city before him, he was free to make plans for the winter, even peek ahead to spring when finally, he hoped, he'd start running again like he used to do on the Steadfast oval. The world seemed as new as the year.

Coming home to the dark apartment brought back the night of Ann's note and the suddenly empty spaces, but the memory only lifted his spirits further. After three months he'd still replaced none of the furniture, merely found ways to make do with the things he had. The rooms looked airy and purposeful, suited to a streamlined life. As soon as the door swung shut, he unpacked his bag and put away the gifts he'd received, adopting and absorbing his family's tokens of love.

On his first day back at work, a slow-moving storm brought waves of sleet and freezing rain, glazing the eastern third of the state. For three mornings straight he left home twenty minutes early, giving himself time to creep along the sidewalks. Parked cars and stairway railings glittered. Shining streets reflected ice-coated signs. Rock salt gritted underfoot along with chipped and scattered ice. Margaret arrived two hours late one morning, after taking Desmond to the Emergency Room. They'd thought he might have broken his ankle, but it turned out to be a sprain. Only Laura seemed unfazed, coolly sipping her diet soda when the others got in, wearing the flimsy little shoes she called espadrilles.

"Ballet class when I was nine," she explained. "You never lose that lightness on your feet and your sense of balance."

The day after the rain and drizzle ended, leaving salt-stained concrete and breathtaking cold, Matthew sat down with the *Inquirer* over breakfast. Leaving early for work every morning had left no time for such comforting rituals. He hadn't read the paper in a while. He began with the local section as he usually did, and stared at a front-page headline. "Laurel wrestling assistant dies in one-car crash." He set his spoon down and reread the head-line. His throat convulsed. He read the article, the unreal facts registering in clumps. He couldn't shake the feeling that he was reading a private message, intended just for him but for some reason printed in a mass-circulation newspaper. He sat for several minutes, feeling very cold. Then he went to the phone and called Nicky Gervais.

III.

BELIEVING

LIGHT TRAFFIC SPARKLED IN the clear morning air. Sunshine raced down the center guardrail and laid a golden sheen on the road. Beside empty fields the neat barns slid by, hex signs vivid against whitewashed boards. Miles ahead, the Turnpike wound through woods, bored into mountains, and careened down steep curves, but if he kept a steady hand on the wheel he'd be fine. No tires would slip. No vehicles would spin out of control. Driving in January, on bare pavement beneath a mocking sun, was the easiest thing in the world.

He embraced the monotonous road noise, letting the whine and rumble surround him. He welcomed the soothing reflector disks flicking by at regular intervals. He couldn't have borne the faint buzz of train passengers, let alone conversation in a car. Of course Nicky had suggested they drive to Stanton together, but Matthew turned him down. He couldn't be tied down by schedules, he'd explained, and the awkwardness of borrowing his parents' cars; but then he admitted that what he really needed was to be alone. The solitary day on the road would do him good.

"I understand," said Nicky. "We all get through these things in our own way. Me, since I got the news, I've had to be around people every second. If I sit and think about it I'll just start bawling."

There was a silence on the line.

"So I guess I'll see you there," said Matthew. "Thanks for filling me in about everything."

"Sure, man. See you there. Drive safely."

Had there been a touch of black humor in the words? *Drive safely*. It was all they could do now, a kind of belated rescue effort. Drive safely, except it didn't matter now. In a way, throughout these senseless first days, driving helped Matthew feel closer to Ben, as if he were sharing in his final act. Matthew was twenty-four. He didn't know the first thing about grieving. He didn't know what people did, how they got through.

He'd gone to work that first morning, the searing headline still fresh in his brain. He didn't know which he dreaded more: his colleagues' sympathy if they knew, or having to tell them if they didn't. The news still hovered in an edgy twilight, available but not yet widely known. When he entered the office Laura looked up at him with a routine smile. Gabe waved, on the phone with someone. To reach his desk Matthew needed to walk past Margaret's office. Without planning to, he paused at her door.

She sat at her desk, her head in her hands. She looked up at him with reddened eyes, stood and came to him. She took his hand, drew him into the room, closed the door. She wrapped him in her arms. He could feel her weeping. This was how it would be, he thought. She would be the one to express his grief for him.

But then she was holding him while he cried and cried.

"I know, baby," she said. "I know."

After a long time she said, "Come. Sit." He obeyed while she sat down across from him at her desk. She looked at him, her eyes still bright with tears. When she didn't look away he felt like she was monitoring him, making sure from minute to minute that he was all right.

She must have decided he'd gotten through the worst of it, because she leaned back and said quietly, "You remember what I told you about Ben."

"You said that God put him in my life."

She nodded. "Now I'm almost sorry I said that. It's going to be hard for you, trying to understand why he's gone. It's going to be very hard." She looked at him for another few moments. "I'm sorry, Matthew."

"There were things he wanted to do," Matthew said slowly. "Like maybe find a church. Take communion. Was he ever baptized? I don't know. And I think I still had things to learn from him."

"I'm sure you did."

He shifted in his chair. "It seems wrong to even think about that. I don't want to feel sorry for myself."

"Well then *I'll* feel sorry for you," she said. "It's awful what happened to Ben, and it's awful what happened to you, Matthew. You've lost a friend you counted on for something important, right?"

He nodded.

She looked at him, perfectly motionless. This time he could tell she wasn't just watching him. She was thinking. "Keep listening," she said. "Sometimes people go on teaching us things after they're gone."

After a long silence he took a deep breath, and managed something like his workplace voice. "I'd like to go to Stanton for the funeral. Actually, I've already made plans."

"Of course. Take as much time as you need."

Those were the only arrangements he'd needed to make at work. He was grateful. He'd had other bosses who would have made everything harder. Even with the Steadfast Rock library staff, those murmuring women who fussed over him like a spare set of aunts, he'd felt nothing like Margaret's compassion. Her blessing went with him as he faced the Turnpike and everything that lay ahead.

He reached his parents' house just in time for dinner. Afterwards they all sat down in the living room, just as they'd have done any other time he visited. To Matthew's relief, no one blurted out how nice it was to see him again so soon. He could tell that they wanted to sympathize. He could also tell that they didn't know how. Ben hadn't lived in their world. They couldn't assume it was all right to say the usual things.

"I forget whether you've mentioned this," said his mother. "Did you have a chance to talk with your friend about the Lord?"

"Ben," said Matthew. "We talked a lot about the Lord. That's why we were friends."

"So he understood about the plan of salvation?"

"Of course."

"Then that must be a comfort to you."

"I don't know," said Matthew. "I think a lot about what I still had to learn from *him*."

"Oh!" said his mother, a little sharply, and got up to pour the tea.

Matthew said he needed to make a phone call, and went into the family room. Under the gaze of Buswell and Machen he sat at the desk where his mother wrote checks. He looked up a number in the little Stanton directory.

"Is this Mrs. Cameron?" he asked when a woman answered.

"Yes."

"My name is Matthew Lindley. I was a friend of Ben's."

"Yes, I remember your name," she said after a pause. She spoke clearly but in a hushed, controlled voice, as though measuring out her strength.

"I'm sorry if I'm calling a bit late. I just got to Stanton a little while ago, and I wanted to . . . I guess I just wanted to say how sorry I am, and how much Ben meant to me."

"Would you like to come over?"

"Now?"

"We have a few people here, it's nothing formal. Really it's a comfort to see anyone Ben knew. His father and I would love to meet you."

"Okay," said Matthew. "I can be there in a little while. Could you tell me how to get to your house?"

A few minutes later he was back in the car. He had forgotten how dark the roads were at night, but at least they were all familiar. During the few years he'd driven in Stanton he'd been to most of its neighborhoods, besides being taken by his parents on church errands when he was younger, and for rides to friends' houses. His headlights led down hills and around sharp bends to a part of town like the one where he'd grown up, with old houses and sprawling yards that no one fussed over very much. Many had vegetable gardens in back, or right out front by the mailbox. The Camerons' two-story home was surrounded by several tall spruces, and had a big open porch. Two or three cars were parked alongside the driveway.

A dog barked when he rang the doorbell. He heard Mrs. Cameron shushing it. With a loud gusting sound the inside door swung open, and a wet nose collided with the storm door glass. Matthew stepped into a tumult of slobbering snout and buffeting tail, while Mrs. Cameron, fingers hooked in a collar, spoke alternately to Matthew and the dog.

"Down, Tucker! No, Tucker. Sorry. He thinks you came to see *him*. Tucker!"

She took Matthew's coat and he walked into the living room, where a group of adults sat in silence. A tall, solidly built man rose, said he was Ben's father, and named the aunts and uncles in the room. Mr. Cameron's handshake hurt Matthew's hand, as though his grip knew nothing of the sorrow and exhaustion in his face. Matthew sat down, hoping he wasn't taking Mrs. Cameron's chair. Tucker, a barrel-shaped golden retriever mix, sat at Matthew's knee getting his ears scratched. Everyone sat and watched Matthew pet the dog. Mrs. Cameron, perched on the piano bench, turned out to be a slim brunette woman, her short straight hair just beginning to go gray. She and Mr. Cameron looked like athletes who'd suddenly turned into slack, slumped versions of themselves.

"Ben told me the reason he didn't have a dog was that he was on the road too much," said Matthew. Tucker butted his paused hand. Matthew continued scratching the dog's ears and knuckling his bony forehead.

"That was the reason he gave, huh?" said Mr. Cameron.

"Ben and Tucker had a complicated relationship," said Mrs. Cameron.

An aunt asked, "You visited Ben's home in Laurel?"

"Yes," said Matthew. "Just this past September. We kept in pretty close touch over the last few years," he went on. "We barely knew each other when we lived here." The aunt nodded, but Mr. Cameron looked puzzled.

"I knew you and Ben were friends," he said. "But I never understood exactly how you hit it off after high school, since you went to different colleges and everything."

Matthew saw that the subject couldn't be avoided. "We bumped into each other at my college, Steadfast Rock. We discovered we were both Christians, and that was when we found we had things in common."

Mr. Cameron nodded, frowning.

"And they say people aren't supposed to discuss religion," joked an uncle.

"I guess that's what they say," said Matthew. "Maybe Ben and I were the exception that proves the rule."

Another silence set in. Tucker lay down with a contented groan, his head resting on Matthew's foot.

"Our family has never been particularly religious," said Mrs. Cameron.

"So the service tomorrow . . .?" Matthew began.

"Just a simple memorial service at the funeral home," she said.

"Burial of the ashes will be in the spring," said Mr. Cameron. "A small family ceremony."

"Will you come to the reception here tomorrow?" asked Mrs. Cameron. "After the service?"

Matthew said he would. Tucker rolled his eyes up at him, tongue lolling.

When Matthew got home his parents were finishing in the bathroom, calling goodnights down the hall. It felt like family camping trips when he was little. He and Miriam settled down to bowls of cereal at the kitchen table. They gossiped about Ebenezer and Steadfast people, discussed the aspiring figure skater two houses down, debated whether anyone big like

Bruce Springsteen or the Rolling Stones would ever play the Civic Arena in Pittsburgh. Miriam said, "Not likely, Mrs. Pikely" in a gruff British accent, the way she used to do when she was thirteen, and they both cracked up. One of the cereal boxes had only a small amount left, so they split it and poured more milk. The mantel clock struck eleven-thirty.

In the darkened hall, pausing outside her bedroom, Miriam whispered, "What did you mean, you had things to learn from Ben?"

He tried to remember making the comment. His thoughts felt sluggish after the long day. "We both learned things from each other," he said. "It wasn't just me learning from him. I think Ben was curious about what it was like growing up the way we did, going to church all the time. And I was learning from him what it's like, being a Christian who *doesn't* go to church."

She seemed confused, so he said, "You know, like when Paul went off by himself before joining up with the other apostles. For a while it was just him and God. I think Ben spent the four or five years after his conversion that way."

She shook her head. "It sounds really strange to me. I don't know what I think about that." She hurried on, "I'm really sorry it happened, Mattie. It's so horrible. I never had a friend who died."

"I never did either. Before."

He lay in his old bed, surrounded by old shapes and shadows. When he closed his eyes he saw taillights, big yellow teeth, a pink tongue, Mrs. Cameron's bent head. Prayers came to mind, the prayers of a child, simple and thoughtless. Good enough for a start, he supposed. He tried to move on to his usual requests, but Ben's absence bulked in his path. Words seemed petty, inadequate, futile. He stopped. Nothing else came. That would have to do, for now. His mind fell silent, a silence lengthened in reply, and he slept.

Late the next morning he drove to the funeral home. Stanton had two, he knew from growing up in the town. He hadn't been inside either one. The two funerals he'd attended had been in churches, and his parents hadn't brought him to the "visitations." He thought vaguely that the place the Camerons had chosen must be the fancier establishment, with its gabled stories overlooking a frozen lawn, enclosed by a low stone wall. The parking lot was full, and he circled several blocks before finding a space. Wind bit his cheeks as he walked back to the building.

He had to sling his coat up onto a heap atop the overflowing rack. After passing through the vestibule, he entered a large space with three rooms opening to each side. He guessed the small rooms were for viewings and funerals, while the larger area served as a sort of concourse and lobby. But on this day over a hundred folding chairs, most of them already occupied, filled the large gathering space. Masses of flowers and a lectern stood at the front. Matthew took a seat in the next-to-last row of chairs.

Immediately he noticed the thick necks. Wrestlers' necks. There must have been more than thirty of them, of different ages, straining the cinched ties and tightly buttoned collars. With stoical expressions the men gazed at the lectern, hands dangling at their knees. Scattered among them sat a few older couples, a number of less athletic-looking college students, a few mourners close to Matthew's age. He'd braced himself to meet some high school classmates, but saw only two or three people who looked familiar. He spotted Coach Watson toward the front. Beside him Nicky Gervais twisted around in his seat, caught Matthew's eye, and nodded.

At eleven o'clock a middle-aged man wearing an expensive-looking suit walked to the lectern and introduced himself as Art Floyd, a friend of the Cameron family. He said the Camerons would be grateful to hear from anyone who would like to say something about Ben. It would be his privilege to begin.

He spoke first about the tradition of athletics in Ben's family. Mrs. Cameron had been a champion tennis player in college, where she met Mr. Cameron, a basketball star. They had instilled in Ben the values of discipline, hard work, and competition. If that sounded severe or even harsh, Art Floyd hastened to add that the Camerons had delighted in giving their son a loving, laughter-filled home. Above all, they taught him to serve and care for others. As teammate, coach, and friend, Ben had demonstrated these virtues in ways that exceeded his parents' hopes. Those in attendance would hear from many people who had experienced Ben's kind and selfless nature. Floyd himself had witnessed Ben's strength of character and his willingness to help in any emergency. It was Ben who drove Floyd to the hospital when he fell from a stepladder and broke his arm.

After Art Floyd's speech, a stream of Ben's teammates, student wrestlers, and coaching colleagues spoke—even several men who'd wrestled and coached against him. His high school and college teammates praised his toughness and determination. People who'd known him later, however, spoke of other qualities. They recalled his patience and a sense of calm in difficult circumstances. He'd struck them as having a kind of inner peace.

"When I first met Coach Cam," said a junior Laurel wrestler, "I knew I could learn a lot from him. He had all that winning experience on the mat, and he had a gift for explaining technique and strategy. Man, that guy could teach you how to get out of *anything*." He shook his head. "After a while, though, I looked up to Coach Cam for other reasons. I could tell he really cared about me, for one thing. But it was more than that, even. He had this—I don't know, *spirit*—that made you want to be around him. He accepted people. He didn't worry about things. He made you feel like everything would be all right. Even now, I feel like, somehow, it's going to be all right."

Was this the Ben whom Matthew had known? The portrait still seemed incomplete somehow. He wanted to think that when people recalled a peace and contentment in Ben, they were describing, without realizing it, his new life as a Christian. But Matthew wasn't sure he believed that. It sounded too perfect, too much like the old Bitter Gulch Boys books. Even when the speakers referred to a spiritual side of Ben, Matthew didn't think he recognized his friend. Somehow the Ben he knew eluded all of these tributes. He thought about going forward and saying a few words. Ben's parents might appreciate it. But anything he added would have felt out of place. And in fact he had no idea what to say. That Ben had a knack for talking about Karl Barth? That Ben had reminded him, at times, of the Apostle Paul? He kept silent, holding fast to the Ben he knew.

Finally Mr. Cameron rose and thanked everyone who'd spoken. His voice trembled slightly as he acknowledged all the support the family had received. After thanking everyone again for being there, he sat down. He said nothing about the reception following the service, and it occurred to Matthew that he'd been invited to a somewhat exclusive occasion. It didn't bring Ben any nearer, but at least he felt he'd been embraced by the family.

A burst of recorded string music signaled the end of the service. People rose, talked quietly, moved slowly toward the back. Matthew stood by his chair. After a few minutes he walked forward, against the flow. He nodded again to Nicky Gervais, then looked away, as though he were searching for someone. He reached the front where, scanning the flowers, he noticed a small arrangement from Ann Clyde. He looked at the flowers and the little card. She would have needed to go to some trouble to do that. He would say something to her when he got home. In another few minutes the front of the room had emptied, except for a young woman who lingered near the first row of chairs. On a small table stood a framed recent photograph of Ben, perhaps a publicity shot from the athletic department. From the back of the room Matthew hadn't been able to see it very well. He walked over and stood before it now.

It was a good picture, with the old fight showing in the slightly narrowed eyes, the center-parted hair left over from high school. Confident smile. Square jaw. The lean and seasoned look of a pro. You didn't need a league, Ben. Or a million-dollar contract. You were your own kind of pro. Coach Cam.

It was time to do what he'd come to do—what needed to be done, and wouldn't be done without him. He understood that now. He took one last look over his shoulder. The young woman still stood there. He turned back to the photo and took a step forward. Raising his right hand he spoke aloud, moving his hand down, then back and forth.

"In the name of the Father, and of the Son, and of the Holy Spirit. Amen."

From behind him he thought he heard a soft "Amen." He remained standing for a minute with his eyes closed, then looked once more at the picture. When he turned around the woman was gone.

He didn't want to arrive too early at the Camerons', so he had a cup of coffee at an out-of-the-way diner, hoping to avoid people from the funeral who'd had the same idea. It took fifteen minutes to get to the place, so he thought he'd have it to himself. Knowing his way around Stanton had its advantages.

He'd guessed right. It was an early Wednesday afternoon, and the diner was nearly empty. To his surprise he felt hungry, so he ordered a sandwich, and soaked up the steamy warmth and the smells of coffee and grilled meat. Two waitresses in mustard-colored dresses and white aprons served meals on thick, heavy platters. He thought he might have gone to high school with one of the women. He ate his sandwich and drank his coffee, staring out the window at gray streets and buildings, white sky. An old lady, bundled in woolen layers, walked a limping collie past the window. Across the street a man swept salt from the sidewalk.

He expected the reception to be hard. He wouldn't know anyone, and would be completely out of place among the sports people. He decided that he'd stay for half an hour, an hour at most, then leave for Philadelphia. He'd talk with Nicky, say goodbye to Mr. and Mrs. Cameron, and be on his way. He felt a little better once he'd made a plan.

When he reached the Camerons', the street was already lined with cars. He walked in after knocking once, and someone pointed him toward a bed where he threw his coat. Returning to the living and dining rooms, he found groups of people talking and laughing in loud voices. He knew this was what happened, but he couldn't help it, he was shocked. He ladled himself a cup of punch, selected a muffin, and hoped Nicky was there. Tucker must have been banished to the basement, poor guy.

The assistant coach, spotting him as he left the refreshments, came to greet him. Matthew set down his muffin and shook hands. More than anyone he'd seen that day, Nicky was showing the effects. He had dark circles under his eyes, his skin looked ashy, and his dark hair lay in clumps. A slight smile seemed to cost him an effort. For a few seconds he stood gripping Matthew's arm.

"How you holding up?" asked Matthew.

Nicky shrugged. "It's been hard."

"Same here." He motioned toward the chatting guests. "A lot of people came."

"Yeah. That's been nice."

They stood looking around the room.

"How did it happen?" asked Matthew. "The accident. I feel like I need to know."

Nicky nodded. "Of course you do. Or else it won't seem real." He paused and took a breath. "He went out to pick up some things for one of the guys who wasn't feeling well. You know, juice and ginger ale, stuff like that. It's the kind of thing he did."

"In the middle of an ice storm?"

"Yeah. Didn't matter. He lost control on a curve that people around there take a hundred times a year. Any other night, you'd know exactly the right speed you should go, just how you should turn the wheel. That night was different, with the ice. He didn't have a chance. The cops don't think he was going all that fast."

"In the city you could hardly walk anywhere," said Matthew. "Driving out here yesterday, I kept thinking how sunny and dry it was, the roads were fine. If only on that night—"

"I know. It's a bitch, man." Nicky's eyes caught on something across the room. "This thing has turned into sort of a reunion," he said. "There's some people I should talk to."

"I understand," said Matthew. "Thanks for everything."

"I didn't do anything," said Nicky. They shook hands again. "Listen, it was good to see you. Even like this. Look me up next time you're in Laurel."

"Okay," said Matthew.

He watched Nicky join a circle of wrestling types. Then he made his way through the crowd, from room to room, looking for Mr. and Mrs. Cameron. There were a lot of people now. Faces blurred together. Noises throbbed in his ears. He nearly ran into a woman who stepped in front of him—the woman who'd watched while he blessed the photo.

"Sorry," she said. "Could I talk with you for a minute?"

"Are you Lisa?"

She laughed. "I must be famous. Are you Matthew?"

"Yes. You're the girl in the canoe. I saw your picture at Ben's."

"And I heard Ben talk about you lots of times." Perhaps embarrassed, she pushed back a strand of dark brown hair. "Well, now that we've got all that straight. There's a porch in back. It's quieter there and not too cold."

"Sure," said Matthew. "Have you been here before?"

"No. I just happened to notice."

He followed her to the back porch, where four cast-iron chairs with vinyl cushions surrounded a wicker table. The chill felt good after the packed crowd. They sat down on opposite sides of the table, and frankly looked at each other for a moment. She had her hands folded in her lap, her burgundy dress tugged over her knees. Her hair fell straight to her shoulders. Matthew leaned back. The cushion sighed.

"What did you want to talk about?" he asked.

"Oh." She shook her head and looked down at her hands. "I don't know now! I think I just wanted to talk to you after what you did. After the service, I mean. And maybe," she laughed, "I wanted to talk to someone who isn't a wrestler."

"That's funny. I guess I just assumed you're a wrestling fan."

"Not at all. You aren't either?"

"Nope." They exchanged comradely smiles. "How did you happen to know Ben then?" he asked.

"You called me the girl in the canoe," she said. "That pretty much tells the story. A friend of mine who knows some guys on the team introduced

Ben and me at a party last summer. We found out we both liked doing outdoorsy things, but we'd been having trouble finding people to do them with. So we started going hiking, biking, canoeing, a little rock climbing. It was fun."

"Sounds exhausting," said Matthew. "I went hiking with Ben once."

"He was in pretty good shape."

"Do you do something on campus?"

"I work in the Registrar's office."

Matthew hesitated. "I never figured out if you and Ben were dating or serious or what. Maybe it's none of my business."

"I don't think we knew either," she said. "We were at that stage where we thought we'd take our time and see where things went. And then it just stopped." For the first time, her voice faltered. "The past couple of days have been awkward. Difficult. As far as a lot of people are concerned, I'm the girlfriend. But that isn't exactly how it was."

Matthew couldn't see why Ben would display a framed photo of someone who was just a hiking buddy, but he didn't say anything. He speculated for only a second or two about how close they might have been. As she said, everything had stopped, whatever it was.

"I can see how it would be awkward," he said, then added, "You must miss him."

"This might sound terrible, but it's too soon to say."

"I think I know what you mean. It hasn't really hit me yet, either."

She shook her head slowly, looking down. "That isn't quite what I meant." She paused. "I don't know why, but I want to say this right. It isn't that Ben being gone doesn't seem real yet. It's more that I can't know yet how much I miss him when I haven't figured out what he meant to me."

Matthew waited, but she said nothing more. He couldn't think of anything to say.

She looked up. "Your turn. Why were you and Ben such good friends?"

"I thought you knew. We talked about God a lot. Who else would say a blessing over his picture?"

"That *was* kind of a giveaway," she said with a smile. "When I saw you do that, I remembered some things Ben said. Not only about you, I mean. It reminded me of that whole side of him."

"Are you a Christian?"

She showed no surprise at the blunt question. "Ben called me an inquirer," she said. "I'm interested. I liked what I saw of Christianity in him, anyway."

"I've known all kinds of Christians," Matthew said. "I never knew anyone like Ben."

"I can believe that," she said. After another pause, meeting his eyes with a pensive look, she asked, "Was he a saint or something?"

Instead of answering, Matthew followed an impulse. "Listen, I'm driving back East pretty soon. How did you get here?"

"I got a ride with friends."

"Do you want to ride back with me?" He could tell she was startled. "You said you're tired of being around wrestlers, and that it's been awkward. I'm feeling the same way. I'm ready to leave." He hesitated. "We could talk more."

"I *would* like to talk more . . ."

"It's a little complicated, but we can work it out," he said. "Tell your friends and get your things. Then we can go to my parents' house for my stuff, and you can change your clothes there if you want. After that we'd be on our way."

Her face began to light up. "You're making it sound like an adventure."

"Not like canoeing or white-water rafting, exactly. It might be kind of fun, though." He stopped, confused. "Well, not fun, I mean, just—"

"Okay. Let's do it. I'll tell my friends and pick up my bag."

"I need to say goodbye to Mr. and Mrs. Cameron. I guess you'll want to do that too. Maybe after I talk to them." He found himself avoiding her eye. He hadn't said it, but hoped she understood. They wouldn't want the Camerons to see them leaving together. "How about I meet you out in front in a few minutes?"

She slung her purse over her shoulder, then abruptly held still. She wrinkled her nose. "Is this really a good idea?"

"What kind of a guy did Ben say I was?"

"Yeah, okay," she said. "If you put it that way."

He found the Camerons in the kitchen, getting more food ready and talking with some friends their age. When they saw him they dropped what they were doing and came to him. He felt like he'd known them a long time.

"I need to be going," he said. "I'm glad I got to meet you."

"Thank you for coming, Matthew," said Mrs. Cameron. She stood looking at him as if he could tell her something.

"I'll be thinking about you," he said.

"You can pray for us if you like." She smiled slightly.

"We'll need it," said Mr. Cameron.

"All right, I will." Then, for the second time that day—or was it the third?—he followed an impulse, and gave Mrs. Cameron a hug.

He got his coat, went outside, and stood beside the front steps. The light wasn't noticeably fading yet, but had the fragile look of a short winter day. There wouldn't be much daylight for driving. In a minute Lisa came walking fast up the driveway, carrying a small suitcase which she set down at Matthew's feet.

"I'll be right back," she said, and went inside.

He waited for what felt like a long time, then she came out with a tight smile, looking down. "You said goodbye to the Camerons?" he asked. She nodded. They said nothing as they walked up the driveway and along the street to his car. Their shoes sounded loud, scraping the pavement. Matthew carried the suitcase for her, although it hardly weighed anything, and set it in the backseat of the Chevette.

"Can you drive a stick?" he asked.

"I have to drive?"

"Never mind. Just your company will help."

"And there's gas and tolls."

"Nah. Well, maybe."

The drive from the Camerons' to his parents' house reminded him of the night before, when he'd left the sorrowing family and the demanding dog. Suddenly he felt heavy and tired, re-crossing the hilly terrain. He thought of Ben taking these roads when they were in high school, driving to all those workouts and practices. Like Matthew making his countless trips to Ebenezer, Ben would have known every rise and hollow. They became a part of you, those repeated journeys. In the same way, it seemed to Matthew now, a part of Ben survived in the winding routes he'd taken every day. This was where he'd discovered his gift and nurtured it. This was where he'd glimpsed a brilliant future, as victories piled up and scholarship offers came in. Perhaps the seeds of faith had quickened here, some dim awareness that the thrill of combat might not be enough.

"I think I'm getting a feel for where things are," Lisa said, jarring his thoughts. "In a way it isn't that different from Laurel."

"I've been feeling that too, since the time I visited Ben," said Matthew. "The two places feel kind of the same. When it comes to getting to know your way around here," he continued, "your hiker's sense of direction must help you out. Where are you from originally, anyway?"

"I grew up in York, went to Lafayette, got my first job at Laurel," she recited. "Just a Pennsylvania girl through and through."

"Welcome to Ben's and my end of the state."

"Did you and Ben go hiking around here, when you were in school?"

"We didn't really know each other then."

"That's right, I forgot. You got to be friends during college."

"Did he tell you about our wrestling match in gym class?"

"No!"

"Good."

"Come on."

"Maybe later. Here we are. I think my sister's the only one home."

They got out and Matthew handed her the suitcase. Entering the house he called "Hello?" and heard Miriam's "In here" from the family room. She was folding laundry while watching a *Gilligan's Island* rerun, strewing the sofa and chairs with sorted heaps according to an old system she had. She looked up at Matthew in the doorway.

"You're earlier than I expected, Mattie," she said. "How did it—oh! Hello."

"Hi," said Lisa.

Miriam looked at Matthew, a blouse dangling in her hands. She had on sweat pants and a T-shirt, a bandanna over her hair.

Matthew said, "This is Lisa . . ."

"Meador," said Lisa.

"Thanks. And this is Miriam." To Miriam he said, "Lisa and I both wanted to get started for home, so she's riding back East with me. We're just here to get my stuff and change clothes."

"Oh," said Miriam. "How was the service?"

Matthew started to answer, but couldn't find a way to begin, especially to Miriam and in front of Lisa.

"There were a lot of people," said Lisa. "They shared stories about Ben. It was good."

Miriam nodded. Matthew showed Lisa the downstairs bathroom, and went to his bedroom to change. He returned to the family room carrying his backpack and garment bag. His sister looked up again with eyebrows raised, rolling a pair of socks into a ball.

"She's someone I can talk to about Ben," he whispered. "They were kind of seeing each other."

The eyebrows went higher.

"Not very seriously, it sounds like. Anyway I'm just giving her a ride, so cut it out." At a normal volume he said, "When do you go back? Saturday?"

"Uh-huh," she said. "Classes start Monday. I can't wait."

"I remember the feeling," he said.

The old sitcom was making him hungry for the chips and cookies they used to devour with Gilligan or *Bewitched* or *I Love Lucy*. The canned laughter tugged at him, tempting him to stay. He thought about offering Lisa something to eat, but decided they'd better not take the time. Besides, they'd eaten at the reception. They could grab another bite when they stopped for gas.

Lisa returned in jeans, a sweater, and knobby-soled boots. She looked good, the way some people looked better in everyday clothes than when they got dressed up. He sensed Miriam giving her the once-over, then felt her watching him look at Lisa.

"Did I hear something about classes starting up again?" Lisa asked Miriam. "Where do you go?"

"Steadfast Rock," said Miriam.

She said the name in a direct, matter-of-fact way, without the "Could you possibly have heard of it?" upward lilt. Way to go, thought Matthew. It wasn't perfect, but it was still their school.

"The name sounds familiar," said Lisa. "Is that where you went?" she asked Matthew.

He nodded.

"It's a small denominational school," said Miriam.

A silence followed the formal-sounding phrase.

"Well," said Matthew. Miriam's eyes pleaded with him not to use the bathroom, not to leave her alone with Lisa. Something else that could wait until they stopped for gas, he decided. He turned to Lisa. "All set?"

He hugged Miriam and wished her a good semester. She and Lisa exchanged polite goodbyes.

"Tell Mom and Dad bye, and that I had to get back a little early," said Matthew, following Lisa out the door. "I'm sure I'll be back again before too long."

"For a happier reason, I hope," said Miriam.

He arranged Lisa's and his things in the backseat while she settled herself in front. It felt like they'd been in the house for an hour, but the car remained slightly warm. He buckled his seatbelt and glanced at Lisa, who gave him a small smile.

"Okay," he said. "That's done. Now let's drive."

"I've been thinking about it. I really do appreciate you suggesting this. I was ready to get away from . . . everything."

"It couldn't have been easy for you."

"It was okay. Ben's parents were great. But after a while it just felt weird. Anyway, thanks."

"Thanks for coming."

They laughed together. He knew they were thinking the same thing: "This is the strangest date I've ever been on."

First they decided on music. Lisa rummaged through the shoebox full of tapes on the floor, and produced a half-dozen of her own from her purse. After some debate they chose Joni Mitchell's *Blue* from Lisa's collection, and Cat Stevens's *Foreigner* from his.

"This car isn't exactly an audiophile's dream," said Matthew, raising his voice over the road noise.

"We can turn it up."

For a hundred miles or so they listened, replaying songs they liked. The vague yearning of *Foreigner* and the moody sadness of *Blue* chipped away the brave veneer of the service and reception, leaving plain words and ragged feelings. Someone or something was always missing, the songs said. A cruel blow, then painful longing. Not even the engine drone could muffle the raw complaints. When the last note died they said nothing for several miles.

Lights began shining from across the median rail, so Matthew turned on his. Bare trees grew dim. Scoured rock faces turned from beige to brown. The bleak world went dark at the end of a bleak day. Margaret was right, his problem was what to do now that Ben was gone, with so much still to learn. Why embark on an adventure like that, just to end it in the middle? What could he do, alone on a new path?

Beside him in the failing light Lisa's face was a blur. His voice sought hers.

"Where did you and Ben go hiking?" he asked.

"Just places near town. We never went very far."

"Did you go to a state park where the trail led up to a spectacular overlook?"

"You mean where you leave the trail and come out on kind of a bluff?"

"That's it. He and I went there. I think it was his favorite place."

"It was. I'll never forget going there with him."

"Would it bother you to talk about it?"

"I'd like to talk about it. It was an incredible day. The weather, I mean. All the time we were hiking, we heard thunder in the distance. It never rained, but there was a lot of wind, and we had this feeling of being on the edge of a storm. When we got to the top it began to clear. It was sunny by the time we turned off from the trail.

"Then we came out on the rocks and the overlook. I was expecting some kind of a view, but it went beyond anything I imagined. If you saw it in a movie you'd think it was fake. First, these enormous brilliant white clouds just bowled you over, they went so high and were outlined with a blinding light. The sun broke through in slanting rays, just like when you were little and thought it must be shafts of light from heaven. The hills had something misty and unreal about them, reaching off into the clouds. We didn't even see the rainbow for a couple of minutes. Can you imagine? The clouds and the light were so overwhelming that a rainbow was almost like an afterthought."

"I don't really have to imagine," said Matthew. "You've given me quite a picture." The day he and Ben hiked to the bluff seemed ordinary by comparison.

"For a long time we just sat there looking," Lisa went on. "Then it struck me that this was when a lot of guys would, you know, make some kind of a move, while we were sitting in this incredibly romantic spot. I was trying to decide how I felt about that when Ben broke the silence."

She started to laugh. After a few seconds she laughed again. "Sorry," she mumbled.

"Well, what did he say?"

"He turned to me, and he had this awestruck expression on his face. It took a while for him to put any words together. Then he whispered, 'Doesn't it make you want to jump up and say "Glory"?'"

Matthew laughed. He couldn't help it. "I can just hear him saying that. And yeah, it does sound funny, especially if you weren't there. So what did you do? Did you laugh then, at the time?"

"Oh, no! Of course not. He was *transfixed*. At that moment I was almost more scared than anything else. He just looked so wild. But then it was like the vision or whatever it was passed, and he smiled at me. I knew that something beautiful had happened, almost as beautiful as the clouds and the sun and the rainbow."

They sat in the dark car, surrounded by the droning and the measured thuds. A dotted line of taillights snaked ahead of them. A semi roared past, then another. Listening to Lisa's story, he'd unconsciously let up on the gas.

She waited for the second truck to go by, then continued in a musing voice. "I think that to me, that stunning view was mainly clouds and rain and sunlight—just the predictable aftereffects of a storm. I don't mean to sound like I was cold and analytical, but a part of me saw it that way, as just a natural phenomenon. Ben saw something else, though. I really believe he saw the glory of God."

"I believe it too," said Matthew. "By the way, I'm starting to see why he called you an inquirer."

"It was hard not to be, being around Ben."

He nodded in the darkness. That was what he, too, had always noticed about Ben. For Ben, God wasn't a topic of conversation but a surrounding presence, like snow to a skier or water to a swimmer. It was just a question of what terms you and that presence were on, how aware of it you let yourself be.

"I used to equate religion with church," said Lisa. "In my family, the whole point of church—at least it seems this way to me now—was that it kept you from having to talk about God, which would have been awkward and embarrassing. If someone started to talk about religion, you could assume they meant church and you'd be more or less covered. Ben was different. He wasn't someone who went to church. He was someone who'd been with God."

"That's pretty much the way I think about him," said Matthew. "Going to church wasn't enough for Ben. He wanted more. He *expected* more. He thought if you had faith it should bring you close to God somehow."

"You didn't tell me whether you thought Ben was a saint."

Matthew thought about it for a few moments. "Well, he certainly wouldn't have called himself that. And I don't think he was trying to do or be anything out of the ordinary. If that were the case I wouldn't be trying to figure out how to be like him."

"So if Ben was a saint, we can all be saints."

"Yeah. Something like that."

A little while later they stopped at a service plaza. After using the men's room and paying for gas, Matthew waited for Lisa at the doors. Having attended a funeral earlier in the day with a crowd of solemn, well-dressed people, he kept expecting to see a Sunday-like throng heading home from the weekend. Instead a stillness hung over the nearly deserted plaza. Standing near him beside the doors, a middle-aged man in a Phillies jacket waited like Matthew, hands jammed in his pockets. A woman helped a little girl with a gumball machine, palms cupped like a safety net under her daughter's tiny hands. The crash and gong of a video game competed with the piped-in music.

He spotted Lisa walking toward him, carrying a paper bag. She smiled across the wide empty space. He'd been anxious to see her, he suddenly realized. In the darkness of the car, in the hours since they'd met, he'd lost the look of her face. He watched her come nearer, her features growing distinct. Her brown eyes were large and slightly sad-looking, except for when she smiled. Then they shone with a friendly warmth. The nose she'd wrinkled, second-guessing this odd trip, seemed too short and compact for the job. Light shone on her straight hair, and a pair of earrings glinted with her stride. Her smile quickened, verging on laughter, while he stared. Her cheeks still glowed from the brief walk outside, or maybe she'd re-touched some makeup.

"What?" she said, drawing up to him.

"I forgot what you look like," he said simply.

"It's me, Lisa. Here, I got you something." She pulled two candy bars from the bag.

"Thanks!" he said. "My favorite kind."

"I noticed the wrappers on the floor. I got a few other things too, to keep us going. Were you planning on stopping to eat before we get there?"

"I thought you might know a good place near York."

"I'll think about it."

Helped by the break and some food, they pushed on, less oppressed by the night. The traffic seemed lighter, and some stars had come out. By the time he'd shifted to cruising speed, Matthew felt ready to pick up where they'd left off.

"I think you said that, in your family, church kept you from having to talk about God," he began. "With us it was the opposite. God was a whole lot more important to talk about than church."

"I guess I'm not surprised."

"It's almost like people were suspicious of church, even though we went all the time. One of the worst things you could say about someone was that he or she went to church but wasn't really a Christian. That they used church as some kind of front or act."

"So how did people prove they were the real deal?"

Matthew paused, remembering. "I think it came down to what you did *outside* of church. Anyone could pray and be pious on Sunday morning. The test was whether you talked about God at school or at work. And of course whether you read your Bible every day."

"I think Ben read the Bible a lot. He sure seemed to know a lot about it."

"Did he ever quote it? Specific passages, chapter and verse?"

She didn't answer immediately. He could feel her searching through her memory, running over the times with Ben. "No," she finally said. "I can't remember a single time."

"That's what I thought. He didn't treat the Bible that way, the way I was brought up treating it. He didn't use the Bible to prove things or make a point."

"You're right," she said. "I never thought about that. And yet the Bible obviously meant a lot to him."

"I saw it too, that real closeness he had to the Bible. It's one of the main things I was trying to learn from him," Matthew said. "A different way of reading scripture."

"Not so literally?"

He laughed. "People always say that: 'taking the Bible literally,' 'a literal reading of the Bible.' I'm not even sure what that means. For me it's a question of what the Bible is *for*. That's what Ben helped me with."

Lisa was silent. He wondered if he'd offended her.

"Tell me the difference," she said. He could tell from her voice that she hadn't been offended, only curious. "I mean, between Ben's way of reading the Bible and what you grew up with."

"You have to stop me if I get to droning."

"It's a long way to York. Drone on."

"Okay. People I grew up with believed that because the Bible is the Word of God, every word of it has to be true. That 'every word' part leads to the literal reading, I guess. The words mean exactly what they say, and are true exactly the way they appear. No fancy interpretation needed."

"So a snake is a snake, and a day of Creation is a day."

"Yeah, I guess. The main thing is that it's true no matter what anyone thinks about it. It isn't subjective. You could point to it like evidence in court."

"Okay."

"So the Bible ends up being this powerful weapon, almost magical. We believed the Bible was unanswerable, it couldn't be stopped. When people talk about telling others the good news, they mean delivering the truth that's in the Bible, so that they'll be convinced and be saved."

"But unless people live on some remote island," Lisa said, puzzled, "they already *know* the 'good news,' don't they? 'Jesus saves.' It's on billboards, it's on TV, it's a punch line. You see 'John 3:16' on signs at football games. Even I know that verse. How is it news? And how does reading it in the Bible make it undeniably true?"

"Exactly. The thing is, at some level my parents and the rest did realize that. They weren't stupid. They said the Holy Spirit has to make people see the truth of the Bible. That's when the light goes on, so to speak. But here's what was different about Ben. He rejected the whole idea of a book full of objective truths. Actually, he never had that idea in the first place, like I did, so it was more like he just bypassed it. He didn't think you believed because you got convinced by some irrefutable chain of facts and reasoning."

"Why do people believe, then? Why did *he* believe? Did he get a message direct from God?"

"I asked him that, the last time I saw him. They were practically the last words we spoke to each other. He told me about a time he lost a match after a long winning streak, and how that experience taught him to trust in someone outside himself. He quit putting all kinds of demands on himself, and accepted the idea that he could be worth something to God. He said that was his story, and his story was what made him believe. Not reading the Bible and thinking about it. All of that came after."

She didn't reply at first. Matthew watched the taillights recede into darkness, remembering that peaceful Sunday evening, sitting on the platform with Ben. The story about the match, and what it had meant to Ben, seemed as right and inevitable as the cool evening and the fading light. He'd never questioned Ben's last words to him. Now, on a rushing strip of pavement, under a cold black sky, with his friend dead, he wasn't sure. Having a story was comforting, but it didn't guarantee anything. The only guarantee was this cold darkness. Maybe over the last few months he'd just been carried away by some hopeful words in the autumn twilight.

"You knew Ben longer than I did," said Lisa. "I didn't know him during the time before his conversion, before his story changed him."

"Neither did I," said Matthew. "Not really. We only got to know each other after he told me he'd become a Christian. I've thought about it, though. Whether he underwent some kind of change. I listened for it in some of the speeches at the funeral."

"I was listening for something like that too."

"I had glimpses of a different Ben back when we were in high school. He struck me then as tough. Hard. I don't want to say more than that—it was just an impression of someone I didn't know very well. But when I met him again during college I remember being surprised that this intimidating guy with his muscles and quickness had come to have faith, a trust in someone outside himself. It seemed like such a different way to live."

"I can't even imagine Ben as tough or hard," said Lisa. "He was always the coach and teammate they talked about today, a warm, thoughtful person." Suddenly her voice changed, and he heard her turn to him. "Hey—what was that about you and Ben wrestling in gym class? I want to hear *that* story."

Matthew groaned. He'd forgotten he'd brought it up. "All right. It's just your basic gym-class horror story, but over the years, for me at least, it's become more than that. At the end of the unit when we worked on wrestling, our sadistic P.E. teacher gave us a kind of final exam. Each of us had to square off with another guy in front of the whole class. I got matched up with Ben. He was new to the school then, and I had no idea who he was."

"You didn't know he was on the wrestling team?"

"Nope. For all I knew he was just good at *looking* like a wrestler. The teacher blew his whistle and the two of us went at it. Of course I completely forgot whatever I was supposed to have learned from the class, and I just winged it."

Lisa laughed, a high sweet sound, amused yet sympathetic. "How awful! Did he pound you into the mat?"

"I'll have you know it was almost a contest," Matthew said with dignity. "We talked about it at his house, that last time I saw him. This fierce determination came over me. I wouldn't let go. The match or whatever it was didn't last very long, but he told me it went longer than he expected. I just hung on and wouldn't let go."

She remained quiet for a few moments, and the sounds of the car and the road filled up the silence. "You should never let him go, Matthew," she said at last. "Don't ever let him go."

They took the York exit and ate at a diner Lisa knew, where her family liked to go after trips. A brusque silent waitress seated them in a booth, leaving them with coffee and enormous menus. Matthew already knew he would order meat loaf, his standard meal at these places. Lisa got an omelet. While they waited, the highway tension drained away. They drank their coffee and looked around the big room. A group of women ate at a center table, talking quietly. Leftover Christmas decorations glittered on the walls. The waitress was as efficient as she was silent, remembering their smallest requests, whisking dishes away. They discussed how large her tip should be.

They'd both arranged to be off work the next day. They ordered dessert and took their time while the diner emptied. As on so many evenings in the Steadfast dining hall, Matthew felt in no hurry to get on with daily life. Why couldn't they just stay here for another few hours? The coffee tasted good and he'd just gotten relaxed. It was Lisa who glanced meaningfully toward the yawning waitress.

They split the check and got back on the Turnpike. The night was a rushing tunnel again, narrower and darker than the actual tunnels that had borne them through mountains. They adjusted once again to the vibration and noise.

"You said Ben believed because of his story," said Lisa. "Do you have a story too?"

"I've thought about that a lot," said Matthew. "The best answer I can give is that knowing Ben—having known Ben—is my story."

"What do you mean? Is he that much of a guiding light for you?"

Matthew smiled in the darkness. "That's a way to put it, I guess. He'll always be a guiding light for me. But what I meant is that knowing him and the way he lived gives me a reason to believe. My story of getting to know Ben is what I've been looking for to replace all the intellectual arguments. I keep remembering the time he and I met again, after high school. That was when he told me he'd become a Christian. I can still see him beside those library stairs, telling me that."

She said nothing. After a while he realized it was a waiting silence.

"It was a shock, really," he continued. "The little I'd known him before, he'd been completely confident in himself, self-assured to the point of seeming cocky. For someone like that to say he had faith in Christ—it stunned me. I believed it had to be the power of God. And then knowing him started to make a difference in my own life. It was like he'd been sent to me somehow."

"I don't mean to sound like I'm pooh-poohing your story," Lisa murmured. "But hadn't you known converts before? Wasn't whatever happened to Ben what was *supposed* to happen?"

"Of course. He was *exactly* what was supposed to happen. But sometimes that just makes the expected thing all the more shocking. Like when I was a kid and read in a nature book about salamanders. I went down to the stream behind our house and looked under a rock, and there was this black shiny salamander! Just like the book said!"

"Boy, deep down you're really kind of a skeptic," Lisa laughed. "You're surprised when what you believe turns out to be true."

"Maybe," Matthew admitted. "But there was something else about Ben. His conversion was different from others I saw or heard about."

"How so? Because he was such a textbook case?"

"It was real. I could tell as soon as he told me in the library, but then I had time—way too short a time—to see how he turned out. His conversion *took*. All those campfire testimonies, and all the people who went forward to see Billy Graham, and all the souls the missionaries claimed got saved—I always figured there was something flash-in-the-pan about all that. Who knew how many of those people would call themselves Christians a year, two years, five years later?"

"You must have known *some* that did."

Matthew shrugged—another pointless movement in the dark. "Maybe so. The really amazing thing about Ben was the *kind* of Christian he became. With some converts, it was like they woke up one day and started spouting a new vocabulary. What changed about them was mainly the way they talked, the clichés and catch phrases they used. Ben *hated* all that."

"Yes! I saw that in him. He really couldn't stand phony expressions."

"Instead he had to find out what was real. He was relentless about it, like in gym class when neither of us would let go. I never knew anyone like him, who wasn't ashamed to say 'Jesus is my savior,' but who took that as the starting point, a mystery to explore, and not the magic formula that ended discussion."

"Is that what you're going to miss most about him? That relentlessness?"

"Yeah. We won't keep finding things out together. He won't be there to push me."

Another long silence followed. This time he knew she was crying.

After several minutes he asked if she'd like to listen to more music. He got her to find Rod Stewart's *Never a Dull Moment* in the shoebox, and they sang along with "You Wear It Well," laughing at each other when they got the words wrong. Suddenly it was time to exit and make their way to Laurel. With Lisa navigating, they got there sooner than Matthew had expected.

Entering town after dark, a different way than by train, he felt like he'd never been there before. Stores and signs looked strange. The streets held no memories of his visit. Lisa directed him to a campus neighborhood with more apartment buildings, restaurants, and bars than he remembered seeing around the guest house. Late-night diners and drinkers strolled the sidewalks. He parked in the lot of her mid-rise building, near the entrance, and got out to fetch her suitcase from the backseat.

"Such a gentleman," she said, taking it.

They stood facing each other outside the building entrance. It was the kind of spot where a lot of people were likely to pass by, even late at night. He wondered why he'd bothered turning the engine off.

"You going to be all right?" he asked.

She nodded. "Just a little tired. It's been a long day. I've only been to two or three funerals before."

"People our age aren't supposed to go to funerals."

"Oh," she said abruptly, and fumbled in her purse until she found a tiny notebook. She scribbled on a page, tore it out, and handed it to him. "Call me, okay?"

"Okay." He tucked the page into his shirt pocket.

If she'd kissed him just then, it would have felt routine, obligatory. A mere goodbye. Instead they remained standing a few more seconds, smiling at each other.

"We'll see each other some time?" he said.

"Soon, I hope."

"I don't know which end of a canoe is which."

"That's okay. We can just drive around and listen to music."

"That sounds nice. Good night."

"Good night, Matthew."

She'd given him good directions from Laurel to Philadelphia. He drove home over empty roads, his mind busy and alert. A little after one he unlocked his apartment door and walked in to an oppressive silence. The kitchen light threw down a harsh glare. His breakfast dishes sparkled in the drainer. When he tossed the mail on the table a letter stood out from the junk, addressed in Ben's spiky hand. He stared at it, thinking over the past few days, trying to sort out what he might have dreamed and what he might be dreaming. Finally, assuring himself that the letter was real, he sat down and opened it.

It was dated one day before the crash. As usual he skimmed the tournament news and the talk about books and movies, impatient to get to the last paragraph, the important one. He read the handwritten lines twice, slowly. He sat at the table a long time, thinking, the way he always did. The sitting and thinking felt so familiar, he had to remind himself that this would be the last time. He waited for it to seem true. Then he folded the letter and returned it to its envelope. He would have to remember to bring it to work. Margaret would want to see it.

Do you make New Year's resolutions? I made one this year, after I read in Romans where Paul prays that God will "fill you with all joy and peace in believing." I guess you can't really "resolve" to have joy and peace when they're supposed to come from God, but I want to at least be ready for them, and dwell on them when they come. I want to experience joy in believing. This made me think of you, because you often talk about how, when you were growing up, people said you needed to know God and know you were saved. Something about that kind of knowing strikes me as worried and grim, compared to joy in believing. Knowing is something I accomplish when I concentrate on a problem and finally figure out the answer. Believing is something I'm privileged to do—something that brings me joy. I'm going to pray for you this year (a second resolution, I guess) that you will have joy in believing.

Keep hanging in there, bro. Hope to see you soon—
Ben

www.ingramcontent.com/pod-product-compliance
Lightning Source LLC
Chambersburg PA
CBHW06080825062
47162CB00005B/1707